MERLE HAGGARD, BONNIE OWENS & ME

FUZZY OWEN
WITH PHIL NEIGHBORS

Published by
Owen Publications
PO Box 842, Bakersfield, CA 93301
www.FuzzyOwen.com

The Library of Congress Cataloging-in-Publication Data Applied For

Fuzzy Owen—
Merle Haggard, Bonnie Owens, and Me

p.   cm
ISBN 978-1-7333881-0-8
1. Personal Memoir   2. Music   3. Celebrity   I. Title
2019

Printed in the United States of America

1 3 5 7 9 10 8 6 4 2

Book design by White Horse Enterprises, Inc.

For interviews or information regarding special discounts for bulk
purchases, please contact Phil Neighbors at pneighbors@valleybaptist.org

DEDICATION

To fans of Merle Haggard, Bonnie Owens,
and The Bakersfield Sound. Thank you all.

TABLE OF CONTENTS

INTRODUCTION

RAY MCDONALD WAS A CLOSE friend of Merle Haggard's. For years, he was Merle's personal assistant and bus driver. When Ray was in high school, he actually lived with Merle, Bonnie Owens, and her two sons, Buddy and Michael. Ray shared the following story with me, and I liked it so much that I wanted to include it here.

In 2015, the Kern County Museum relocated the famous Haggard railroad boxcar home from its location in Oildale, California to the Pioneer Village in Bakersfield where the house was to be restored, and placed on permanent public display. Merle Haggard, his family, and a large crowd of fans gathered for a dedication ceremony at the boxcar's new museum location. When Merle stood to speak, he noticed Fuzzy Owen, his life-long friend and personal manager standing in the crowd.

Merle's first words were, "None of this would have ever happened if it was not for Fuzzy Owen." Ray was standing next to Fuzzy, and he noticed that Fuzzy had not heard what Merle just said, so he repeated it to him.

"He's not blaming me for all this, is he?" Fuzzy asked.

Later that day, when they were back on the bus, Ray related the story to Merle, and they both laughed and laughed about Fuzzy's comment.

In many ways, Fuzzy can be blamed for Merle Haggard's career and success. Fuzzy, of course, did not write "Mama Tried" or sing "Silver Wings," but he was the man behind the music for one of the greatest country artists of all time. Fuzzy was on the bus, in the studio, and by Merle's side at every concert he performed. All told, they spent more than fifty years working together almost every day of the week.

If you are looking for a "kiss and tell" book about Merle Haggard, this is not it. Fuzzy has no desire to be negative, because that is just not who he is. When we sat down together to write this book, Fuzzy insisted over and over that we must tell the truth and nothing but the truth, and that is what we have tried to do. Over the years, there has been a great deal written about Merle Haggard, and you may find that some of Fuzzy's stories do not always agree with what others have written. When I asked Fuzzy about those differences, he always said, "Well, I was there!" So, that settled it for me. The center of the country music universe in the 1960s and 1970s was Bakersfield, California, and Fuzzy Owen was right there in the middle of it. This is Fuzzy's story.

Phil Neighbors
Valley Baptist Church
Bakersfield, California
July, 2019

"Well you could do better,
but you won't do bad in Bakersfield."
—from "Beer Can Hill"
(written by Merle Haggard and Manuel Abraham, Jr.)

FOREWORD

Sing a Sad Song: The Ballad of Fuzzy and Merle

I DON'T REMEMBER EXACTLY WHICH day in March of 2016 it was, but I was at home, the phone rang, and I noticed the call was from area code 503. Maybe someone is calling with news on Merle, I thought. I answered and was surprised to find it was Merle himself.

"What are you doing?" he asked.

I said, "Sitting here looking at Connie Smith."

He replied, "Ain't you lucky."

"Where are you?" I asked.

Hag said, "I'm in a room in California that you, Jimmie Rodgers, and I would probably call a prison cell."

"Is the sun shining there?"

Merle said, "Very little these days." He then went on to say, "I just wrote one you might want to hear."

That was an old routine of ours. Hag would call me from time to time and try out new songs he'd written. When he did that, it made me feel ten feet tall. I always cherished those calls, however, this one was different. There was no creative spark about it, or the excitement of needing someone to hear it. It was unsettling.

"What's it called?" I asked.

In a weak and raspy voice, Merle introduced his new song as "My Last Escape." Then, there was silence on the line for what seemed like an hour. Finally, from his hospital room in California, Hag told me his words.

It was hard to take because I somehow knew that one of my dearest friends in this world was calling to say good-bye. Goodbye in the language of a song. A song that said what needed to be said without putting a chill in the room. Hag struggled, but he got his story told. When he finished telling me the words to "My Last Escape," I was leveled. I told him it was a masterpiece, which it was. Straight from his heart.

Merle then said, "When I get out of here, maybe you and your band could come out here to my studio and we'll record it."

"Just tell me when," I said.

Hag signed off with, "Take care of that lady that you love." I love you's were spoken, then the call was over.

In just a matter of a few days, Merle was gone.

Not too many hours after the news of Merle's passing, I received a call from his attorney, Ray Green. Mr. Green informed me that Merle had planned his service, and my and Connie's presence was requested. A couple of days later, we traveled alongside many others to Palo Cedro, California, taking our love to the Haggard family. The day of Merle's homegoing was underscored in tears, stories, and music. I kept a strong heart about me, and will be forever grateful to the eagle that floated above the service, giving everyone gathered a reason to look up.

I remember saying that afternoon, "As long as there's a radio, Merle will be with us. As long as there is country music, honkytonks, jukeboxes, or country bands who need real songs to play and sing, Hag will remain. He is part of the atmosphere. His words and melodies dance alongside the very air in which we breathe."

Hag's big day was sealed with one of God's patented California sunsets.

A few months later, my band, the Fabulous Superlatives, and I, played a concert in Bakersfield at the Fox Theater. We shared the bill that evening with Merle's sons, Benny and Noel, along with Hag's legendary band, the Strangers. That afternoon, during sound check, unannounced, Fuzzy Owen walked through the door.

Everything stopped as we gathered around Fuzzy. Fuzzy *is* Bakersfield, California. He is country music aristocracy, a king among men, a beloved monarch of twang and a true statesman—as well as one of the founding fathers and master architects of the West Coast country music empire. He is *the* contributing inventor of the California sound.

Everyone was glad to see Fuzzy. There was a lot of handshaking, storytelling, reminiscing, and general goodwill in the midst of Fuzzy's presence. After a time, Fuzzy being Fuzzy, in his all business-like manner said, "I know you boys need to get to work." He stood and listened to Noel, Benny, and the Strangers for a while. He then asked me about the ticket sales for the show, looked around the theater and said, "Well, I guess I'd better go."

I asked Fuzzy if he wanted to come see the show, but he said, "Naw, it's okay."

I walked with him out the stage door into the alley behind the theater. We shook hands and Fuzzy began to walk away. Watching Fuzzy Owen walk into the distance could have been the closing scene of a movie where the hero disappears into the sunset. As I stood and watched Fuzzy, my heart called out and the tears for Merle and the Strangers finally came. I suddenly realized the permanence of it all, the end of an era. If Hag had been inside the Fox Theater, Fuzzy wouldn't have been leaving. I studied him as he walked, and thought, that man is probably the best friend Merle Haggard ever had.

From the first song Hag ever recorded until the last, Fuzzy was there. They were closer than brothers. Fuzzy and Merle made it up as they went: songs, records, bands, buses, hits, misses, deals, girlfriends, wives, kids, true love, and false alarms. They proclaimed the fire of youth, middle age, old age, the passing of the trains, the changing of the guard, the vanishing of old America, endlessly crisscrossing the nation, helping carve out a road for the likes of me to travel upon. They tore it up at honkytonks, roadhouses, auditoriums, coliseums, stadiums, the White House, and all points in between. The two of them shared the spoken, the unspoken, the heaven and the hell of it all.

They knew all of the old rhinestoned ghosts, as well as the multitudes of night birds who followed their shows and lived by the brand of country music they were peddling.

Fuzzy could reason with Merle when no one else on earth could. When the door was closed and the two of them were talking, everyone in the inner circle knew it best to stand clear until that door opened again. Merle knew Fuzzy had his back and would bail him out of anything he'd gotten himself into. However, on the morning of April 6, 2016, not even Fuzzy Owen could bail Hag out of his appointment with the Angel of Death. It was a pre-destined matter, one we all must face. I've since wondered if their story turned out the way the two of them envi-sioned. Regardless, it's hardly any of our business, but we got to be a part of it anyway. In a sense, every song Merle sang told their story, and that told us all we really need to know.

As Fuzzy faded out of sight that afternoon in Bakers-field, I thought of something Merle once said to me. "One of these days Fuzzy is going to be wrong, but so far, that hasn't happened."

With love to Fuzz and Hag,
Marty Stuart

PREFACE

IN 1972, AFTER YEARS OF producing concerts for some of the biggest rock 'n' roll acts in the world, acts such as the Beatles, the Rolling Stones and Bob Dylan, I decided to return to my country music roots. So, I asked the people at Capitol Records who they thought was the country music performer that had the greatest future. Without pause they said, "Merle Haggard."

I scheduled a meeting with Merle and his manager, Charles "Fuzzy" Owen, in Bakersfield, California. We immediately hit it off. When the meeting was over we shook hands, with the agreement that I would produce and finance all of Hag's live performances, except Lake Tahoe and Reno, Nevada. That meeting changed my life. I was about to spend the next ten years with a man I think is one of the most talented country music singers and writers in history.

Here was a man who was raised in a boxcar, lost his father at the age of nine, escaped from thirteen institutions by the time he was eighteen years old, spent two years and

nine months in San Quentin State Prison, and in 1970, became the Academy of Country Music's entertainer of the
year.

Oh, and by the way, I took him to the White House
in 1972 at the invitation of President Richard Nixon.

With the guidance and friendship of his manager,
Fuzzy Owen, and the support of his second wife, Bonnie
Owens, Merle Haggard became the poet of the common
man. Because of his troubled past Merle often went
through difficult times. But I believe he expressed his pain
through his music. If you listen to his music, you hear his
life: "Mama Tried," "The Fugitive," and "Hungry Eyes,"
to name a few.

In the ten years we worked together, I'm proud to say
Merle and I never had a cross word. There have been several books written about his life, but nobody knew the man
like Fuzzy Owen. He was with Hag from the beginning to
the end. Fuzzy was Merle's manager, but most of all, he
was his best friend. So sit back and enjoy the story of one
of country music's greatest artists and writers, told by the
man who helped him survive through the good and the
bad. This is the real story of "The Okie from Muskogee,"
Merle Haggard.

Bob Eubanks
July, 2019

NOTE TO THE READER

"**MERLE HAGGARD AND I WORKED** together for more than fifty years, yet we never had a contract. At different times during those years, I was his steel guitar player, recording engineer, producer, promoter, booking agent, accountant, bus driver, mechanic, personal manager, and always, his friend. I was with Merle from the very beginning of his music career until he passed away in his bus on his birthday in 2016. Along the way, I helped put Merle and Bonnie Owens together in the studio, which created the signature Merle Haggard sound. I had a front row seat to what many people believe was the greatest country music career of all time. This is the story of Merle Haggard, Bonnie Owens, and me."

—Fuzzy Owen

CHAPTER 1

A Boy from Squirrel Hill

MY HOME TOWN IS SQUIRREL Hill, Arkansas, which is located just outside the city limits of Conway, Arkansas, right in the middle of the state. If you go straight west from Squirrel Hill on Interstate 40 you will eventually arrive in Bakersfield, California, which has been my home since I was seventeen years old. Squirrel Hill and Bakersfield are the only two places I have ever called home.

My dad began life as a sharecropper, but during the depression and the war years, he became a successful businessman. One of his real moneymaking operations was to bring whiskey into our dry county and sell it to farmers and other people in and around Conway. He kept up this operation for years, and it was very profitable. Dad never got in trouble with the law (that I remember), but I guess you could say he was a bootlegger. I do know this: he kept food on the table, and took care of his family during the depression.

Dad was a good provider. He took his earnings from the farm and bootlegging, and purchased an auto mechanic garage in Conway. In time, Bob's Garage and Auto Repair Shop began to grow, and he hired a couple of mechanics to keep up with the work. Of course, those in the know understood they could also buy a half pint of whiskey at the back of the garage when they brought their car in for repair. Business boomed!

After a few years, Dad also opened an auto wrecking yard across the road from our home. During World War II, scrap metal was in great demand, and Dad cut up over one hundred cars and sold them to the government for the war effort.

Every day after school, I walked to Dad's auto repair shop, and went to work. I loved working on those old cars. The mechanical skills I learned in my youth were very helpful to me a few years later, in the early days when I was on the road with country music star Merle Haggard, because I had to constantly work on our old buses to keep them going.

Dad also purchased a couple of trucks that we used to haul cattle to and from the sale barns and farms all over Arkansas and Missouri. He built quite an operation. Before I turned sixteen years old I began to drive Dad's trucks, delivering all those cattle. Fortunately, I was never stopped by the police, because I was too young to have a driver's license. Driving Dad's trucks on the winding mountain roads in Arkansas also helped me later, when I drove Merle's buses thousands of miles across the country without a single accident.

I was always good with numbers, and while I was a teenager, I began to keep the books for Dad's business. We had the auto repair shop, the salvage yard, and the trucking company. I learned basic accounting skills and payroll as a kid working for my Dad. This experience, too, was helpful to me later. Early in my days with Merle I played steel guitar in his band, but there came a day when Merle asked me to stop playing in the band and take over the business operations for him. Because of my work as a teenager in my dad's business, it was an easy transition. Through all of our years of business together, Merle and I never had one problem over money, and I kept a complete account of every penny.

From the time I was a child, music was an important part of my life. Our family always gathered around the radio to listen to the Grand Ole Opry on Saturday nights, and we also especially enjoyed listening to Bob Wills. He was very popular in Arkansas, Oklahoma, and Texas. After I met Merle, I realized he was a big fan, too. In fact, he idolized Bob Wills, and we were both thrilled when several of his Texas Playboy Band members traveled with us on the road at different times during Merle's career.

When listening to music, I especially loved the sound of the steel guitar, and my favorite player in those early days was Leon McAuliffe, who was in Bob Wills' band. When I was fifteen, Dad sold a car to a man in Conway, and a guitar was thrown in on the deal. Now, I wanted to learn how to play the steel guitar, just like I heard on the radio, but this was not a steel guitar, just a regular acoustic guitar. So, I removed the plastic nut from the top of the neck, and replaced it with a piece of metal from the garage. This lifted the strings above the fret board, like a steel guitar or Dobro. I then took a wrist pin that connected the rod to the piston in a Ford Model A, and used it for the bar on my homemade steel guitar. My country music career was on its way!

I put my first band together when I was sixteen. We had my childhood friends, Max Fletcher on bass, Doyle Wilson and Bill Dixon on guitar, Nelson Stamps on fiddle, and I played the steel guitar and sang. The problem was, there was not a real demand or opportunity to play music in Conway. On our best night ever, we made four dollars apiece. It didn't take me long to realize I could not make a living playing music in Arkansas.

A solution was at hand, though. My cousin, Lewis Talley, had moved to Bakersfield, California, and told me there were several places there where country music was being played just about every night. Dad also had two sisters living in Bakersfield, so I made up my mind to move to California when I was seventeen. So in 1946, Max Fletcher and I loaded my 1936 Ford, and we headed west on old Route 66.

I rented a little room from one of my aunts and started to look for a job. I soon found work as a busboy at Tiny's Waffle Shop on Chester Avenue in downtown Bakersfield, making six dollars a day. Max got a job playing country music at a place called the Sad Sack on Edison Highway, and they paid ten dollars a night over there. So, I quit my job at the waffle shop, and began my professional musical career playing at the Sad Sack, which was a beer joint with a house of ill repute on the second story. I put together a three-piece band, and we began to play music for them. The problem was, we were all underage and could have gotten in big trouble if we were caught working in a place like that. The owner of the nightclub developed a signal system to alert us when he saw the police coming, and on his cue, we had to jump out of a window behind the bandstand and run away. We must have been fast runners, because we never got caught.

We played at the Sad Sack for several weeks, and then I heard from other musicians in Bakersfield that we could make sixteen dollars and fifty cents a night if we joined the local musicians union. That was not a hard decision at all, and we quickly joined. The Sad Sack did not pay union wages, though, so I found myself out of a job. But I quickly found work for my band at the Blackboard Café on Chester Avenue. I believe we were the first band to play country music at the Blackboard. Prior to us, bands played top forty music. Eventually, the Blackboard became one of the most famous country music nightclubs on the West Coast. We played there for a short time, until I landed us a full-time job at the Clover Club on Edison Highway in East Bakersfield. We became their regular band for the next several years.

Later, musician and DJ Bill Woods put together a great band that played full time at the Blackboard Café. There were a lot of good bands in town then, but I believe the two best were my band at the Clover Club and Bill Woods' band at the Blackboard. Eventually, Buck Owens' band, the Buckaroos, emerged from the Blackboard and

Merle Haggard's band, the Strangers, emerged from the Clover Club.

The country music scene was really coming alive in Bakersfield at that time, because the town was full of Okies, Arkies, and Texans, all of whom loved country music. People in California who were originally from Oklahoma are called "Okies," and people in California, originally from Arkansas, are called "Arkies." The Texan part you can probably figure out. Many of them made good money in the oilfields, and looked for places to eat, drink, and dance after work.

Nightclubs were opening all over town, and they all wanted live country music. Everything was going great for my band and me. Then I got a letter from my mother back in Arkansas telling me that the draft board had contacted her, and was looking for me. That meant I had to quit my job and move back to Arkansas. Uncle Sam was calling, and it was not long before I was off to fight in the Korean War.

CHAPTER 2

Korea: A Christmas from Home

WHEN I WAS DRAFTED, THE army sent me to Fort Chaffee, Arkansas for boot camp. That was fine with me, because it was very close to my home in Squirrel Hill. Several years later, Elvis Presley was also inducted into the army at Fort Chaffee. Boot camp went by quickly, and next thing I knew, they had shipped me off to the front lines in Korea.

The army had an outfit at that time called Special Services, whose purpose was to entertain the troops. Along the way, I met a fellow Arkansas native named Ray Jones who played fiddle in the country band with the Special Services. Ray and I became good friends, and we maintained contact through all these years. When Ray got out of the army, he played fiddle for country music legend Hank Thompson for many years.

During the war, I played steel guitar with his band several times at the officers' club, and really wanted to join their band and play music during my army career. The

army had other ideas, though, and turned down my request to join the band. They decided I should be shooting
a machine gun in Korea instead of playing steel guitar in
a country band.

After boot camp was over, I was placed in the 3rd Infantry
Division, 7th Infantry Regiment Company C. I was proud
to be a part of the 3rd Infantry Division, as it is one of
America's greatest fighting units. Audie Murphy, the most
decorated soldier in army history (and who later became
a well-known actor), was numbered among the ranks of
the 3rd Division during World War II.

They placed us on board a big troop-carrying ship,
we set sail for Korea, and it took about a week to get there.
One thing I learned very quickly was that I would have
never made it in the navy. I was sick aboard ship all the
way across the Pacific. Every time I smelled food I got sick,
and had to lie down in my bunk. Years later, I was concerned about my inability to travel well over water when I
traveled with Merle and the band on a big cruise ship. Fortunately, I did not get sick aboard that ship, but still, I was
happy to get back on land.

Everywhere I went in Korea seemed to be either up-
hill or downhill. Our job in the infantry was to take the
high ground and hold it. My outfit had to do this several
times, and the worst part of the fighting was always at
night. We'd be dug in on top of a hill with our machine
guns in place, then the enemy would charge our position

over and over again. The army would light up the night sky with huge flares, and we fired away. I still cannot figure out why those North Korean soldiers just kept coming up those hills. So many of them were killed.

Not long after being in Korea, I received my first promotion, and became the radio operator for my company commander. I was fascinated by the electronics of the radio, and my experience with sound equipment back at the Clover Club in Bakersfield helped me operate the radio for my captain. When I got out of the army, and really got going in the music business, I built three different recording studios and helped record some of country music's greatest hits, so my experience in the army had an unexpected long-term benefit for me.

I served as radio operator for several months, then was promoted again and began to drive a truck. We were constantly trucking food, ammunition, and other supplies to the guys who were in the thick of the fighting. In fact, one of my closest calls with death came when I was driving supplies to the front. We were stuck in a tight spot on a road when our convoy came under heavy mortar fire, and the enemy was walking their mortar shells right down the road toward my position. I jumped out of my truck to try to find better cover, but there was nowhere to go. Each mortar round came closer and closer. Finally, the rounds stopped, just before they reached my truck. I have never been more afraid in my entire life than I was that day when I was stuck in that convoy. Religion was not important to me during my younger days, but I realize now that God was watching over me that day in Korea.

Christmas, for a soldier on the front lines, can be a tough time. I only experienced one Christmas in Korea, but still remember how lonesome I felt. I wrote my first song that Christmas, and it reflects what I felt that holiday. I titled it "Christmas from Home."

I am thinking of Christmas and a happy New Year
That is coming to my home and I won't be there
There will be laughter and cheer, but I'll be alone
There is nothing so blue as a Christmas from home

Christmas from home, is lonesome you see
I often wonder will they think of me
I am thinking of them, but I am so alone
There's nothing so blue as a Christmas from home

I made it through that cold and lonesome Christmas in Korea, and my tour of duty soon came to an end. The army sent me back to Fort Chaffee where I finally ended up playing music at the officers' club until I mustered out of the service. When I finally got out of the army all I wanted to do was to get back to Bakersfield and play music.

CHAPTER 3

Meeting Bonnie Owens

ONE PERK OF MY DAD'S thriving business was that he bought a new Ford car every year. So, while I was still in Korea, I wrote my mother and asked her to tell Dad not to trade in his car when he bought a new one this year, that I would buy it from him when I got home. Dad never drove his cars hard, and he always took great care of them. I purchased his one-year old 1951 Ford Victoria with the money I sent home from the army. When the army finally released me, and after a short visit with my family, I loaded my Victoria and headed back to Bakersfield. A couple of years later I booked my band on several shows in Alaska, and drove that car all the way there and back.

Before I left Arkansas, though, I called Thurman Billings, the owner of the Clover Club, and asked if I could return to my job that I had before I joined the army. He said, "Absolutely," and in short order, my band and I were back in business, playing music.

Mr. Billings and his wife often had lunch at a drive-in hamburger joint on Union Avenue. In time, they became good friends with a young carhop who worked there named Bonnie Owens. Mrs. Billings particularly liked Bonnie, and they offered her a job as a cocktail waitress at the Clover Club. So, Bonnie quit her job at the drive-in, and went to work for the Billings.

Bonnie was originally from Oklahoma, and at that time was married to a young country singer named Buck Owens. When she went to work at the Clover Club, we quickly found out that her husband was not the only talented member of her family. Bonnie could sing. Really sing. The patrons at the club loved her voice and asked every night for us to "let Bonnie sing."

I was just getting my record label, Tally Records, started, and wanted to record Bonnie, because I felt she had a great chance of making it big in the music business. We recorded several singles with Bonnie that climbed into the country charts, including "Why Don't Daddy Live Here Anymore," "That Little Boy of Mine," and "Waggin' Tongues." Bonnie signed with Capitol Records, and one of her highest chart-topping singles was "Stop the World and Let Me Off." We used future Steel Guitar Hall of Fame member Ralph Mooney on steel and Bakersfield's own Gene Moles on guitar on that record. These were two of the best musicians in the business.

Bonnie was later dubbed the Queen of the Bakersfield Sound. Bob Eubanks, Merle's booking agent and concert promoter, and long-time host of *The Newlywed Game*, said of Bonnie, "If ever an angel came down from heaven and walked among us, it was Bonnie Owens." Everyone loved her.

Bonnie also could sing with anyone and make them sound good. If you don't believe that, listen to a duet Bonnie and I did in 1954 called "No Tomorrow." We recorded that song at RCA Victor Studio in Los Angeles, and used Buck Owens and my cousin Lewis Talley on guitar, Jelly Sanders on fiddle (Jelly was a fantastic fiddle player from Oklahoma, and Bob Wills' first cousin), and Bill Woods on piano. All of these musicians lived in Bakersfield, which was quickly turning into a national hotbed for country music. I was thrilled to be part of what was happening, but had no idea that we all were just getting started.

CHAPTER 4

"Dear John Letter"

HILLBILLY BARTON WAS A SINGER and songwriter from Bakersfield, California who wrote a very sad song called "Dear John Letter." The story is about a soldier on the battlefield who gets a letter from his sweetheart informing him that she is leaving him, and is going to marry his brother. Hillbilly traded the song to my cousin Lewis Talley for his 1938 Kaiser car. Lewis then sold half of the song's publishing rights to me for two hundred dollars. I still own a third of that song today.

In early 1953, Bonnie and I worked up an arrangement for the song, and recorded it on a small independent label, called Mar-Vel Records. (I hadn't quite gotten Tally Records ready.) We released it on several local radio stations, and it received a great deal of radio play in Bakersfield. I also sent it to a disc jockey friend of mine in Little Rock, Arkansas where it went to number one in their local market.

When Ferlin Husky, an established country singer from Bakersfield who enjoyed considerable success with Capitol Records, heard the song on the radio in Bakersfield, he approached us about recording it. He wanted it for a young singer named Jean Shepard, who was from nearby Visalia, California, and had recently signed with Capitol. In the spring of 1953, we traveled to the Capitol Records studios in Los Angeles and cut the song. So, we used Lewis Talley and singer/songwriter Tommy Collins on guitar, Bill Woods on piano, Jelly Sanders on fiddle, and I played steel. We tried several guitar players, including Buck Owens, who was a fantastic musician, but none produced the sound we wanted. Finally, I worked out an arrangement with my cousin on the introduction where he and I played note for note on his acoustic and my steel.

Ken Nelson, the country music producer at Capitol Records, placed the song on the B-side of the record thinking that the A-side, "I'd Rather Die Young," would have more success. But by June, "Dear John Letter" was number one, and had also crossed over to the pop charts. The song stayed in the charts for weeks, and eventually sold over a million records. We were all so excited that "Dear John Letter" was a smash hit!

Some consider "Dear John Letter" to be the beginning of the Bakersfield Sound. I don't know about that, but it certainly was the first big hit to come out of Bakersfield, but in the years to come, many more followed.

That one song also threw open the doors for Jean Shepard's career. She moved to Nashville, and in 1955, was invited to join the Grand Ole Opry. Eventually, she was inducted into the Country Music Hall of Fame. All of this began because we bought Hillbilly Barton's song for a 1938 Kaiser worth four hundred dollars.

Before the end of the year, we were back in the studio at Capitol to record a follow-up single to "Dear John Letter," called "Forgive Me John." In a short time, it climbed into the top ten on the charts.

We were all happy for Jean's success, but her career path was not the model that other Bakersfield country artists would take. Most of the successful Bakersfield musicians and singers stayed in California, rather than move to Nashville, as Jean did. There were plenty of opportunities for us right here in Bakersfield, and with Capitol Records eventual support behind us, it just made sense to stay in California.

After the success of "Dear John Letter," Ken Nelson began to use me, and several other musicians from Bakersfield, for studio work on a regular basis. I played on dozens and dozens of Capitol recordings as a studio musician. I played steel guitar in the studio for Ferlin Husky, Joe Maphis (one of country music's flashiest guitarists), Buck Owens, and numerous other country artists. Buck Owens used me on steel guitar for his original version of "Down on the Corner of Love," and Tommy Collins used me on bass guitar on all his Capitol recordings.

Several nightclubs were going strong in Bakersfield in the 1950s and 1960s, and I played in every one of them.

On Edison Highway, there was the Clover Club—where I spent most of my time—and Bob's Lucky Spot. On Chester Avenue, there was Tex's Barrel House and the famous Blackboard Café.

Bakersfield also had several large dance halls that booked country music acts on a regular basis. The Beardsley Ballroom in nearby Oildale had been a great venue until it burned down in 1951, and Bob Wills played there several times a year. On the south side of Bakersfield was the Rainbow Gardens, and the Pumpkin Center Barn Dance. Some of country music's great stars performed in these locations.

My band and I were playing music all the time, and between our regular jobs in the clubs we also traveled down to Los Angeles to play in the studios. The music business is work! On Sunday afternoons, we played in jam sessions before our regular jobs with our own bands in the evening. That allowed us to play with different musicians, and make a little extra money. We were playing six nights a week and twice on Sunday

I was now making a good living playing music in both Bakersfield and Los Angeles. Meeting and working with so many top artists and musicians in the 1950s and the early 1960s also helped prepare me to record a young Merle Haggard in the studio on his first recordings.

The musicians in Bakersfield were a close-knit group of people. We all worked together, and I never sensed any jealousy among any of us. We were all willing to help each other any way possible. We filled in for each other, recommended one another for studio work in Los Angeles, and played in each other's bands. I believe this attitude created an environment that made the Bakersfield Sound grow and thrive. There was a huge number of musicians and singers who emerged from Bakersfield, and they changed country music forever. Bakersfield became the center of the country music universe, and I was right in the middle of it!

CHAPTER 5

The Cousin Herb Henson Show

IN THE EARLY 1950S, SEVERAL daily country music television shows began to appear on the local network stations in Bakersfield. Many of these were live radio shows that crossed over to the new medium of television. These included *The Jimmy Thomason Show*, *The Cousin Herb Henson Trading Post TV Show*, and later, coming out of nearby Fresno, *The David Stogner Show*. David was known as "The West Coast King of Western Swing," and he co-hosted the show with his band, The Western Rhythmairs. Television stations were looking for talent to fill their local time slots, and country music shows were being played everywhere.

Herb Henson hitched a freight train to Bakersfield from East Saint Louis, Illinois, and decided to seek his fortune here. By chance, he rented a small house from one of my aunts, and got a job picking up and delivering clothes for a local dry-cleaning company. Herb was a piano player who often stopped by to play piano at the Clover Club, where I worked in 1953. It wasn't long before "Cousin" Herb landed his own country music television program that had a very successful run. He adopted the "Cousin" moniker from another country artist from Bakersfield.

Herb also was the station manager of a country music radio station in Bakersfield that eventually became KUZZ, which became one of the most successful country music radio stations in the country. The KUZZ radio call letters are a tribute to Cousin Herb Henson. Today, this radio station is owned by Buck Owens Enterprises.

As soon as *The Cousin Herb Trading Post TV Show* (which aired daily not only in the Bakersfield area, but up and down the central coast and valley of California) launched, Herb offered us a job as the house band. Bonnie Owens, of course, came along with us. She soon became a favorite with the television audience, just as she was at the Clover Club. In addition to Bonnie and me, there were a number of different players in the Trading Post band, but the primary band members were Lewis Talley, Roy Nichols (who later became the lead guitar player for Merle Haggard), Al Brumley, Jr. (son of the great gospel songwriter Albert E. Brumley, who wrote "I'll Fly Away" and "Turn Your Radio On"), and Herb Henson.

Every day I played music on the Cousin Herb television show, and each night I played at the Clover Club. When a musician plays music hours and hours a day, he or she gets good at their craft, and during those days I had hundreds of songs memorized. Each day before we played the Cousin Herb show, we took maybe ten minutes to write up a playlist, and decide how we would play each song.

There was no need to rehearse, because we were playing all the time.

Cousin Herb's show was a live, forty-five-minute show that aired five days a week. We only played forty-five minutes, because any longer than that, Herb would have had to pay us union wages. The show was worth it for my band and me because we could promote when and where we were playing that week. Country music was still red hot in California. A fan could hear country music on the radio up and down the state, and it seemed like there were country music nightclubs in every town. The television shows helped promote the popularity of country music, and as a result, we usually played to a full house at every show.

Local country music shows helped set the stage for the national country music shows that appeared on television in the 1960s. Buck Owens had one of the early nationally syndicated country music shows called the *Buck Owens' Ranch Show*. He filmed the show in Oklahoma City at the WKY television studio, and was one of the first to have a country show recorded in color. Buck invited Merle and his band, the Strangers, to perform on his show while I was still playing steel guitar with the band. There is a great video clip of us playing "I'm a Lonesome Fugitive" on Buck's show that is available on YouTube. Other national shows like *Hee Haw*, *The Glen Campbell Good Time Hour*, *The Johnny Cash Show*, *Barbara Mandrell and the Mandrel Sisters*, *The Porter Wagoner Show*, and the *Ozark Jubilee* later provided country music to a huge new audience.

Cousin Herb booked country music's greatest stars on his show when they toured in California. I remember playing for artists such as Tex Ritter, Bob Willis, Lefty Frizzle, Johnny Cash, George Jones, Tennessee Ernie Ford and many more, on the Trading Post show. Just about every country singer of any significance played the Cousin Herb show during those years, and, our musicians from the Clover Club were the back-up band for all of them.

Herb Henson was a fantastic emcee. He had a quick wit and could sell anything. It is tragic that not one single taped program of the Trading Post show has survived. Apparently, the television station reused the tapes over and over, until they became useless. Cousin Herb did as much as anybody to promote country music in Bakersfield.

On the tenth anniversary of the Cousin Herb show, Capitol Records produced and recorded a live album at the Bakersfield Civic Auditorium (now the Rabobank Theater and Convention Center). The show featured many of the country artists that recorded on the Capitol label. The house was packed to hear stars like Buck Owens, Tommy Collins, Jean Shepard, Joe and Rosa Lee Maphis, Johnny Bond, Glen Campbell, and Roy Clark.

I played steel guitar with Cousin Herb's Trading Post band, and we served as the stage band for those country stars on that historic recording. The album, *Country Music Hootenanny*, provides a great example of Herb Henson's emcee skills, and you can hear his signature song, "Y'all Come," at the beginning of the recording. That record truly is a piece of country music history.

Sadly, Cousin Herb unexpectedly passed away of a heart attack shortly after the recording of his tenth anniversary special. He was only thirty-eight years old.

CHAPTER 6

Tally Records

MY COUSIN LEWIS TALLEY WAS quite a businessman, and started Tally Records in 1954. Not long after he started the company, he talked me into becoming part owner. In time, I became the sole owner because Lewis had to sell out due to personal reasons. I still own the Tally label today. Our first studio had really cheap equipment, so we only recorded demo records in Bakersfield. When I needed to record a song that I wanted to release on the radio, I drove to Los Angeles, or went over to Las Vegas to use better studio equipment.

One of the earliest songs I recorded was the Buck Owens' tune "Hot Dog." which released on Pep Records in 1956. Buck and I had met in the early 1950s in one of the many nightclubs in Bakersfield, we worked together on numerous recordings as studio musicians at Capitol Records. "Hot Dog" is a real rockabilly song that Buck released under the name of Corky Jones.

The lead guitar work on "Hot Dog" was done by Buck himself, and I played steel guitar on the original recording of that song. As I noted earlier, Buck was a fantastic guitar player, and was an A-list studio musician for Capitol Records for many years. "Hot Dog" came out right when Elvis was hitting the charts, and the rockabilly-style of music was really becoming popular. Tally records provided a new opportunity for me to be involved in the thriving music scene that was emerging in Bakersfield.

The first time I ever heard anything about Merle Haggard was at the Tally studio in 1957. Lewis told me a teenage singer had stopped by with a demo single that I needed to hear. Lewis really liked his sound, and thought we should consider signing him. I listened to the demo, and he was good, but he sounded exactly like Buck Owens.

"We do not need another Buck Owens, because we already have one," I said.

Lewis and I discussed it for quite a while, and eventually decided not to record Merle. Years later, Merle told me that he was crushed when I turned him down, and that his feelings had really been hurt. He was discouraged, because he thought getting his demo to Lewis and me was his one shot at getting a recording contract.

Sometimes I still cannot believe that I turned Merle Haggard down the first time I heard his demo. But, it turned out that my denial was not the end of the road for Merle and me.

One Sunday afternoon in 1963 at Bob's Lucky Spot, I was playing with the first band of the jam session. When we finished, I typically packed up my steel guitar, and headed to the Clover Club for my job that night. For whatever reason, that day I packed up my steel, but stayed in the club to listen to the second band that was playing. That afternoon, Merle Haggard was playing bass in Jelly Sanders' band, and he also sang a couple of songs. You may recall that Jelly was a great performer and studio musician who played fiddle on countless recordings at Capitol Records. He was a big part of the success of country music in Bakersfield.

But, the bottom line that day was I could not believe what I heard when Merle sang. He sounded nothing like the demo I had listened to a couple of years earlier. When the band finished its set and Merle came down from the stage, I approached him, and said, "That was the best d . . n singing I have ever heard."

"Well why don't you record me?" Merle asked.

"Okay," I agreed. "Let's find a song."

The fact that I owned Tally Records was the reason Merle and I began our work together. I put him in the studio as fast as I could after hearing him sing the second time at the Lucky Spot nightclub. We made country music history on that small independent Bakersfield recording label, and that is how Merle Haggard's recording career got started.

CHAPTER 7

Merle Finds Us a Song, a Sad Song

WHEN I HEARD HIM SING at the Lucky Spot, Merle had just gotten out of San Quentin State Prison. He was not proud of his years in prison, and felt he had shamed his family, who were all God-fearing people. For the longest time following his days in San Quentin, Merle was jumpy when there was a sudden loud sound, or when someone moved quickly around him. He always had his guard up to protect himself.

On one occasion, just before we went into the studio for the first time, Merle was caught shoplifting at a liquor store. When I heard about it, I spoke to the owner of the business and asked him not to press charges. I was fearful that this could be a big problem for Merle, and that he might be sent back to prison. The owner cooperated with us, and we worked it out among ourselves. Thankfully, we never had a problem like that again. Prison life is not easy to get over.

In the early days, there were times when Merle had a short temper, and I had to tell him that he could not speak to people like that. I often had to apologize for Merle to musicians, fans, and the business people in the music industry, but eventually, Merle's attitude began to change. I do not always understand the ways of God in our lives, but I think God must have allowed Merle to go to prison for those two and half years. This may sound strange, but prison changed Merle and made him a better man.

After my conversation with Merle at the Lucky Spot, all we needed was a song to record. While we were looking, Merle went to work for the country artist Wynn Stewart in Las Vegas. Wynn had written a new song called "Sing a Sad Song" that he was about to record. Merle loved the song and asked, "Wynn, you do not want to be responsible for me not becoming a star, do you?"

"Well, of course not!" Wynn said.

Merle then said, "Then let me record 'Sing a Sad Song' and let's see what I can do with it."

Wynn gave the song to Merle, and we got ready to record it. It turned out that "Sing a Sad Song" was the tune that launched Merle Haggard's career.

Wynn was a country star in the 1950s and 1960s and he had several big hits such as "Another Day, Another Dollar," and "It's Such a Pretty World Today." He had a tremendous band that included Ralph Mooney on steel guitar, Roy Nichols on lead guitar, and Merle Haggard on bass. Now that was a pretty good lineup.

When Wynn gave permission for Merle to record "Sing a Sad Song," I told him to bring Wynn's band and meet me at Norms Restaurant in Hollywood. We got to-gether over lunch to talk about the song, then headed to the studio. Merle sang the song perfectly, and what you hear on the studio recording is the very first cut. We were all excited about what we had on tape, and Merle was anx-ious to get it on the radio to see how it would do.

I felt the song needed a big string section on it, but did not have enough money to hire the musicians. I was Merle's producer on those early recordings before Capitol Records signed us. In fact, I was the producer on several singles and albums after we signed with Capitol. A pro-ducer puts up the money for the recording, and in those days I had a very small budget to produce Merle's music. If a producer did not have a contract with a label, he had to pay the studio for the recording time, and also pay the musicians union scale.

I told Merle that "Sad Song" would be a much better single if I could put strings on it, but I needed some time back in the clubs in Bakersfield to come up with that kind of money. In a couple of weeks, I went back to the Los An-geles studio, hired the musicians, and placed those big, beautiful sounding strings on "Sing a Sad Song."

Some say the song has a real Nashville sound to it. Maybe so, but to me that song needed a big, full orchestra sound. Merle always loved smooth singers such as Frank Sinatra, Bing Crosby, and Tommy Duncan. Merle could have been a great big band crooner if he had wanted to sing that style of music, but he was a country singer, and "Sing a Sad Song" is one of the prettiest songs that we ever recorded.

Several weeks after we released "Sing a Sad Song" on my Tally label was when Capitol Records came to Bakersfield to record the tenth anniversary celebration of the Cousin Herb television show. Merle sang "Sing a Sad Song" on that show, but it was not placed on the album because he was not yet a Capitol Records recording artist. However, that was about to change. Our friend at Capitol, Ken Nelson, was the producer on the *Country Music Hootenanny* record. When Ken heard Merle sing, he wanted to talk, and it was not long before Merle Haggard became one the biggest selling artists for Capitol Records—in the same era when both the Beatles and The Beach Boys were with them.

Capitol Records played a crucial part in the success of Bakersfield's country music. We were close enough to Los Angeles to easily record our music there, and they had the resources to push our West Coast country sound all over the nation. Having Capital Records behind us allowed us to remain in Bakersfield and make our music. If there had been no Capitol Records, whose studios were only about a hundred miles south of Bakersfield, we would have been forced to take our music to Nashville to play and record. That would have changed everything, and there might never have been a Merle Haggard. Cousin Herb Henson, and Ken Nelson at Capitol Records, were a big part of the success of Merle Haggard's music and of the Bakersfield Sound.

When Ken wanted to sign Merle to Capitol, I guided Merle through the contract signing process, and made sure he got the best deal possible. I warned Merle to not sign the first offer they made. "Do not sign anything without me being with you," I said. Sure enough, they approached Merle when I wasn't around and tried to get him to sign.

Fortunately, Merle said, "I need to talk to Fuzzy." We did get Merle a much better deal when we sat down with Capitol together. Over the years Ken Nelson became a good friend to both of us, and we had a great working relationship. He always allowed us to use our own musicians, and arrange our own songs. He was the perfect producer for our music.

Merle and I were very proud of "Sing a Sad Song," and we put everything we had into it. I have always felt that it is one of Merle's best songs, and it was our first single that made it onto the charts. I knew that our first song would either make us or break us. We were both always so grateful that Wynn Stewart gave us that song.

CHAPTER 8

My Favorite Merle Haggard Song

WE DID NOT USE MANY of Merle's own songs on our first album, because he was just beginning to write. Before Capitol signed us, we had recorded six songs on my Tally label, but we needed six more to complete the album. We had to find more songs, and find them fast! Fortunately for us, there was a wonderful group of country songwriters in California at that time who were available to us. We selected songs written by Ralph Mooney, Tommy Collins, Red Simpson, and Liz Anderson to finish *Strangers*, Merle's debut album.

The title cut for the album was "(My Friends Are Gonna Be) Strangers," co-written by Liz Anderson and her husband, Casey. Liz was originally from Minnesota, but had been living in Sacramento, California. She wrote, or co-wrote several songs for us including "(I Am a) Lonesome Fugitive," which became Merle's first number one hit. She wrote that song after watching the popular 1960s television show, *The Fugitive*. Liz was also a Grammy-nominated country music performer, and the mother of country music legend Lynn Anderson, whose 1970 hit "(I Never Promised You) A Rose Garden," written by Joe South, was one of the most popular cross-over hits of all time.

Over the years, Merle recorded over eight hundred songs on seventy different albums. Any artist needs help from a lot of different songwriters to record that many songs, and we were fortunate to have some of the best.

So, in 1965, we were hunting for songs, recording songs, and trying to put a band together. Everything was moving so fast that we had not yet given the band a name. I was actually relieved when Red Butler, a disc jockey on **KAFY**, a local radio station, asked if his audience could help name Merle's band. He proposed that we play the front and back side of our Tally label single, "My Friends Are Gonna Be Strangers" and the Tommy Collins penned song, "Sam Hill," and let the audience choose between the names Strangers and Sam Hill Boys. We agreed, and our hometown fans chose the name Strangers. The people of Bakersfield were the first to hear Merle Haggard on the radio, and they gave the band its name.

The *Strangers* album was a big hit, and reached the top ten on the *Billboard* country charts, but we knew we needed several follow-up hit songs to keep the momentum going. As mentioned, Merle's first hit single, "Sing a Sad Song," was written by Wynn Stewart, and his second hit single, "My Friends Are Gonna Be Strangers" was written by Liz Anderson. At the time, Merle had not yet written any songs of significance, but that was about to change, because in

1965, he wrote "Swinging Doors" and "(Tonight the) Bottle Let Me Down." Those two songs demonstrated that Merle Haggard was not just a great singer and performer, but that he was also becoming one of country music's greatest songwriters.

People often ask what my favorite Merle Haggard song is. Well, that is a tough call, because there are just so many good ones. But I always come back to "Swinging Doors." That is the first song Merle wrote that was a big hit, and it stayed in the country charts for almost a year. I love "Swinging Doors" because it paid the bills for us.

In those early days, as producer, I put everything I owned into Merle's music, and was ten thousand dollars in debt by the time the song was released. That was a lot of money in 1965. In our contract with Capitol, I sold all of Merle's recordings that we had done on my Tally label to Capitol, and with the success of "Swinging Doors" I was able to get out of debt. I never regretted or worried about the money I invested in Merle's career, because I just knew that Merle was destined to be a star.

Merle and I did have a difference of opinion about what we should title his first self-penned single, the song that became known as "Swinging Doors." He wanted to name the song "Here 'til Closing Time" taken from a line in the song:

> Stop by and see me
> Anytime you want to
> 'Cause I'm always here
> At home 'til closing time

I suggested that the better title would be "Swinging Doors," which is also taken from a line in the song:

And I've got swinging doors
A juke box and a bar stool
And my new home has got
 a flashing neon sign

"Swinging Doors" became a huge hit for us, and it probably did not make any difference what we titled the song, but it is now, and forever will be, "Swinging Doors."

I am also often asked how many number one songs Merle recorded. The answer is thirty - eight. That is truly an unprecedented number, and I don't know if any other country artist has ever matched or exceeded it. To put this in perspective, Hank Williams had eleven number one hits and Buck Owens had nineteen.

I also like to respond to that question by pointing out how many number two hits Merle had. A number one hit is wonderful and can define an artist's career, but a number two, or even a top ten hit, might make more money, because it all depends on how long a song stays in the top ten.

For instance, "Swinging Doors" never made it to number one, but it stayed way up in the charts for almost a year. You never really know how much difference there is between a number one or a number two chart topping song. And there might just be a few less record sales between them. What I learned real quick was that we wanted a song to stay on the charts for as long as possible.

A good example of this is Merle's number one hit, "Legend of Bonnie and Clyde," which shot up the charts to number one, but soon came down and was out of sight. The B side to that single was "Today I Started Loving You Again," which never made it to number one. However, that song stayed in the top ten for months and months. Merle often said that "Today I Started Loving You Again" was his biggest hit, because it has been recorded hundreds and hundreds of times by other artists.

Keeping Merle at the top of the charts quickly became my number one goal, and I found a helper in that in our own back yard. Her name was Bonnie Owens. Even though I had been working with Merle, I hadn't neglected my work with Bonnie. When I started with Merle, Bonnie was well on her way to having her own great solo career. For example, in 1965, Bonnie was named female vocalist of the year at the very first Academy of Country Music (ACM) awards show. But then, with Bonnie's full support, we teamed her up with Merle.

When I first put Merle and Bonnie together in the studio in 1965, it was pure magic. And, the public and music industry wholeheartedly agreed. The next year, in 1966, Bonnie and Merle received the ACM Duet of the Year for the song, "Just Between the Two of Us," written by Liz Anderson.

In my opinion, the best Merle Haggard songs have Bonnie singing on them. Their voices fit perfectly together, and we were able to take Merle and Bonnie's music to the bank over and over again. All in all, Bonnie sang with Merle for more than thirty years.

There was also magic between Bonnie and Merle in the live shows. We had started to tour Merle, because the more people he could get in front of, the more records I knew we would sell. At that point in time, though, Bonnie was still working her own shows, too. In 1965 I booked Bonnie on a package tour to Alaska with several other Capitol Records artists. Merle found out about it, and took off to join them. I was surprised to receive a phone call from Merle while he was in Alaska telling me that he and Bonnie were going to be married.

Merle and his first wife, Leona Hobbs, had divorced in 1964. They had four children (Dana, Marty, Kelli, and Noel), and Bonnie, of course, had been married to Buck Owens from 1948-1953, and had two boys (Buddy and Michael). I did not see Merle and Bonnie's marriage coming, just as I did not see their divorce coming, more than a decade later in 1978.

When they got home from Alaska, I loaned them my Chrysler station wagon and they drove back east to play several shows. Their honeymoon was driving across the country on a concert tour. Over the next few years, Merle and Bonnie, and my wife Phyllis (whom I had married in 1960) and I, became close friends, in part because we were all beneficiaries of the success of Merle's career.

During those early Merle shows, I discovered that Merle had an uncanny ability to imitate the singing style of different country singers. He could sing and sound just like Hank Snow, Marty Robbins, Johnny Cash, Buck Owens, and many others. For years, Merle used this ability to entertain the crowds at his concerts. You could close

your eyes when he sang their songs, and swear it was actually those country stars who were singing. Whereas before,
Merle's ability to sound like Buck Owens, for example, was
a negative on a demo record intended to launch Merle's
career, now the ability was a great crowd pleaser and
helped fill out Merle's shows before he had enough songs
of his own.

Later, Merle found his own voice and became, in my
opinion, the greatest country singer ever. Grand Ole Opry
star Whispering Bill Anderson, who certainly knows something about country music singers, once told me that Merle
was his all-time favorite singer. George Jones and countless
other country artists have told me same thing.

CHAPTER 9

The Hits Kept on Coming

EVENTUALLY, MERLE WROTE ALL KINDS of songs: prison songs, truck songs, gospel songs, and of course, honky-tonk songs. One of his best honky-tonk songs was the 1966 single "(Tonight the) Bottle Let Me Down." This was an important song for Merle because it was a top ten follow up hit to "Swinging Doors." There are a lot of "one hit wonders" in country music, so it was important for Merle to demonstrate that he could keep the hits coming. Fortunately for all of us, "Swinging Doors" and "(Tonight the) Bottle Let Me Down" were just the beginning of what was to come. Of the more than eight hundred songs that Merle recorded, one hundred and ten of them made it into the top ten in the charts.

However, Merle and I had a difference of opinion on how "(Tonight the) Bottle Let Me Down" should be recorded. He wanted to have a big string section on the song, but each song is different and this was not "Sing a

Sad Song." I remember saying, "No, no, no, Merle! We need the steel and Fender Telecaster guitar, like we used on 'Swinging Doors.' People are just now beginning to hear your songs, and they need to become familiar with your sound."

I had learned that trick from Ken Nelson on Jean Shepard's music. After convincing Merle how the song should be recorded, we used Ralph Mooney on steel guitar and James Burton on lead guitar. Merle's usual guitar player, Roy Nichols, had a previous commitment that did not allow him to play on that particular session, so that is why we used James Burton. James is a legendary guitarist who went on to be inducted not only into the Rock and Roll Hall of Fame, but the Rockabilly Hall of Fame, and the Musicians Hall of Fame and Museum. Ralph Mooney ended up in the Steel Guitar Hall of Fame.

The combination of those two incredible musicians produced one of the very best instrumental openings to any song Merle ever recorded. When people ask what the Bakersfield Sound is, I tell them to listen to "(Tonight the) Bottle Let Me Down." James Burton had been the guitar player for Ricky Nelson, then worked for Elvis Presley for many years. We used James on several of Merle's recordings, including "Mama Tried," and he also played the amazing guitar solo on "Working Man Blues."

"(Tonight the) Bottle Let Me Down" helped define Merle's sound, and it gave us that all-important follow up hit an artist needs to keep the momentum going. The good news, which we did not realize at that time, was that Merle was going to have a string of hits that seemed to never stop.

In time, Merle moved away from honky-tonk songs, and began to write songs that came from his own personal experience, songs such as "Mama Tried" and "Branded Man." His songwriting was just getting started and the hits just kept on coming.

We were blessed to have the best steel and lead guitar players in the world playing on these recordings. That is one reason why Merle Haggard's music sounded so good then—and still does. We eventually stopped using James Burton on our recordings, because after he began to work with Elvis, he began to demand double and triple union scale to play on a session. We still had plenty of other excellent guitar players to choose from, though.

The use of the steel and Fender guitar solos became the foundation for Merle's early music. Ralph Mooney was the greatest steel guitar player that I had ever heard. Now, that is no offense to Merle's usual player and band leader, Norm Hamlet. Both he and I agree that Ralph was an innovator on the steel guitar and had a style all his own. Ralph moved to California from Oklahoma, and played for Wynn Stewart, Buck Owens, Waylon Jennings, and he also played on many of Merle's records. He was an early member of the Strangers and traveled with us on the road until Merle had to fire him.

Ralph was drinking too much, and decided to quit and go back home to his wife, "Mrs. Moon." We told him no, he had to finish the tour, but he decided he would get in the bus and drive home. We were able to stop him before he could drive away, but Merle had to let him go. Later, he apologized to Merle and they made up, but after the tour ended, Ralph never traveled with us again. He did go on to have a long career in country music, before he died in 2011.

Merle first met guitarist Roy Nichols when Roy was playing in Lefty Frizzle band at the Rainbow Gardens Club on Old Highway 99 in South Bakersfield. Lefty had a smash hit in 1950, "If You've Got the Money (I've Got the Time)." Roy had also played for Maddox Brothers and Rose (once America's most popular hillbilly band), and later was a part of Wynn Stewart's band.

Roy developed a unique style all his own that perfectly fit Merle's music. A great example of Roy's guitar style can be heard on Merle's studio recording of "Branded Man." Merle's regular steel player, Norm Hamlet, said that Roy never played a song the same way twice. Each night on stage, Roy seemed to come up with a lick that none of us had ever heard before.

Merle always said the most important part of a performance was the song itself. We both wanted the audience to remember the song. A musician's job with the Strangers was to compliment the singer, and no one did that better than Roy. He always played a song with as few notes as possible. "Less is more," he said, "and you do not have to play everything you know on every song."

For Roy, it did not have to be a hot lick to be memorable. He usually sat next to Norm on the steel guitar when he was on stage. Bob Wills' guitar players often sat, so Merle had no problem with Roy doing that. On stage, Roy never tried to draw attention to himself, and in some ways, he was very shy. He wanted to provide just the right accent for a song, and often, when he finished playing an instrumental break, he just stopped playing altogether, and let the rhythm section carry the tune.

Roy did not like playing rhythm guitar, and Merle knew that. So, in a poker game one time, Merle bet Roy that if he lost the hand, he would have to play rhythm on every song at our next concert. Well, Roy lost, and all during that next show, Merle looked at Roy, and smiled as Roy played rhythm.

CHAPTER 10

Taking Care of Business in the Music Business

WHILE MERLE WAS MY FULL-TIME job. I still kept my hand in with my own songwriting. In 1967, Wynn Stewart recorded my song, "Ole What's Her Name." It was on the B-side of his number one hit, "It's Such a Pretty World Today" on Capitol Records. Now, my single didn't go number one, but Wynn's did—and I was on the B-side! The lyrics to "Ole What's Her Name" cannot be compared to anything like Merle's 1969 hit, "Mama's Hungry Eyes," but I enjoyed writing songs that had a little humor in them. The opening lines of the song is:

> *Well, I'd admit that there been lots*
> *Of pretty girls that I've known*
>
> *There have been lots of Flossie Mays*
> *And Mary Janes*

But there is one that stands out above the others
Oh I'll never forget Ole What's Her Name

Time can never drive her from my memory
No one else could mean so much to me
And ever since she went away
My life has never been the same

Oh I'll never forget Ole What's Her Name

A funny story about that song is that Merle's mother's name was Flossie, and after the song came out, I told Mrs. Haggard that I had written a song about her. She got a big kick out of that. Mrs. Haggard always was such a lady and was a wonderful person.

As Merle's career got going, he wanted to be sure to take care of his band, because he remembered the days when he was a band member with Buck Owens and Wynn Stewart. We tried our best to put the Strangers up in good hotels every night, and each band member received one hundred dollars cash, a day, for food. Most concert venues provided food for the band before or after the show, so each band member pocketed as much of that money as possible.

We also paid the band well, and they made a much better salary than members of other country bands. The Strangers were not getting rich, but they did make a decent living, and that is one reason why so many of them, like horn player Don Markham, along with Roy Nichols and Norm Hamlet, stayed with Merle for decades. Merle liked to tour, so our guys always had steady work. He always wanted the band to shine, and over the years, they recorded five different instrumental albums.

Don Markham played horns for the Strangers for years, and was from Bakersfield. Before he went to work for us, he was in Johnny PayCheck's band. One day while on the road, we crossed paths at a truck stop in New Mexico. Don came over to see us on our bus and began to tell us how bad it was traveling with PayCheck's band. He said there were two brothers in the band who constantly picked fights with everyone else. Don said he couldn't take it anymore, and that he was going to quit when he got back to Bakersfield.

"Don," Merle said, "why don't you come over here and join our band?"

Don got up, went over to PayCheck's bus, picked up his horns and clothes, and got on the bus with us. That was it, and Don Markham played horns for the Strangers for the next thirty years.

Bonnie Owens also toured and sang with Merle and the band for more than thirty years. Merle always encouraged Bonnie to sing solos and duets with him on center stage, and in my opinion, her background vocals are a big part of Merle's signature sound. In 1966 we released Bonnie and Merle's duet album, *Just Between the Two of Us*, on Capitol Records. The album was a big hit, and reached number four on the charts.

Their duet album became the forerunner for other duet acts such as George Jones and Tammy Wynette, and Conway Twitty and Loretta Lynn. We recorded three of my songs on Merle and Bonnie's duet album: "Slowly but

Surely," "I Want to Live Again," and "Stranger in My Arms." Each of these songs featured Bonnie's soaring harmony with Merle's lead. In my opinion, the best example of their vocal blend is on the song, "Slowly but Surely." Merle recorded several more of my songs over the years, but these three were the most on any one album.

After our first album was released by Capitol, we hit the road with the Strangers, and as Merle's success grew, things got busier and busier. Finally, after a couple of years, Merle said, "Fuzzy, I need you to stop playing steel guitar and just take care of all the business affairs for me." That meant we had to find a replacement for me in the band, and I knew just who to call. Norm Hamlet had become a good friend and was an excellent steel guitar player. I had asked him to fill in for me at the Tex's Barrel House on Chester Avenue while we were out on tour. So, I called Norm and offered him the job. He gave the Barrel House two weeks' notice and met us on the road. Norm loves to tell the story that when he finally joined the band, Merle told him that he hoped that they might have a good five year run. Well, that five years turned into almost fifty years of playing music together.

I continued to travel with Merle and the band after we hired Norm to play steel guitar, but in time, I thought perhaps I did not have to travel on every single tour, that I could stay in Bakersfield and work out of our home office. Merle reluctantly agreed, and on the next tour, I stayed home. They were gone about a week when I got a call from Merle. "Fuzzy," he said, "catch the next plane to Minneapolis and get back on tour with me. I need you out here on the road." So, I caught the next plane out and joined the tour, and I traveled with Merle and the band until he passed away.

For years, the only time I was not with Merle and the band was when I stayed behind in a city to mix a song we had just recorded. When Merle wrote a new song on the bus, he always wanted to sing it in the next concert. That was the best test for his songs, because we could see how the audience reacted to it. If the response was positive, and most of the time it was, he wanted to record the song immediately. Because of this, we recorded Merle's songs all over the country. I'd call ahead to the next city down the road, and locate a recording studio. We recorded the song and kept on moving. By the time we finished a tour, we might have two or three new songs recorded. I can't tell you how many number one or top ten hits we recorded like this. Of course, most of Merle's songs were recorded at the Capitol Records studios in Los Angeles, but many others were recorded in studios all across America.

On one concert tour, Merle brought Norm Hamlet and Roy Nichols into his hotel room and set them both down. He told them he needed one of them to become the band leader for the Strangers. Roy spoke up first and said, "Merle, there is no decision to make. I do not want the job. I will carry my own amp and guitar onto the stage, and all I ask for is a place to sleep." Merle then offered the job to Norm, and he became the band leader for almost fifty years.

Many say that the Strangers are the best country band of all time. I believe it, and that is due in no small part to Norm Hamlet. For decades, we opened every show with a Norm Hamlet instrumental as Merle was introduced to the crowd. Norm's job was to make sure the band was set up and ready to go for every show. Roy Nichols was right, Norm was the perfect man for the job, and he is the number one Stranger. Norm's parents were from Arkansas, just like me, and sometimes we still talk about how two Arkansas boys ever made it this far. Someone asked Norm why he stayed with the Strangers for so long, and he replied, "Well, Merle made me the band leader, and I never got around to firing myself."

CHAPTER 11

Life on the Road in Our First Bus

IN THE EARLY DAYS WE traveled on the road in a pickup truck with a camper shell, or sometimes in a station wagon. On one trip I was sleeping in the back of the pickup when some equipment fell right across my bed. I still have a scar on the tip of my nose from that experience. Every time I look close in the mirror, I see the scar, and it reminds me of those early days on the road.

When the band began to grow, though, we had to get a bus. Bob Wills' band was the first to travel in a bus, so we were excited when we got ours. I found a bus for forty-five hundred dollars that needed a lot of work. I had to re-model the inside, so I went down to the local army-navy surplus store and purchased some cots, and installed them in the bus.

On our first road trip, I was still working on the bus as we traveled down the highway. That old bus was nothing like the beautiful luxury buses we traveled in later on, but it did get the job done. We drove that old bus for several years, and were proud of it.

Of course, the bus had no air conditioning, so it was miserable in the summer. We were in Waco, Texas when the heat finally got to us, so I had an idea that we could place a small air conditioning unit on the top of the bus to get some relief from the heat. Merle and I rented a Volkswagen Bug (because it was cheap), and drove to a Sears store in Fort Worth, Texas to purchase the air conditioning unit. Those little Bugs are small, and I was not thinking about the size of the air conditioner that needed to be hauled back. We had a terrible time getting it in and out of the car.

I bolted the unit onto the bus and it worked fine, however, there was a small problem. When the unit ran for a long time, the condensed water tray filled up and when we hit the brakes, the water overflowed. I had placed the air conditioning unit right over Merle and Bonnie's bed, so when the tray overflowed, their bed got soaking wet. Life on the road was not always fun and games.

I worked constantly on the old bus to keep it running. All those years of mechanic work in my dad's garage when I was young came in handy, as that thing broke down all the time. Merle loved to tell what happened one day while I was working underneath the bus trying to repair something that was giving us trouble. A young man approached while I was working on the bus, and asked me, "How do I get started in the music business?"

Merle said I never came out from under the bus, but spoke to the kid as I kept working on the engine. "On

Monday morning," I said, "go out to the Kern and Tulare County line, and get in a race that is run to Nashville. There is a man there who will start the race off with a gun. Then the first one to make it to Nashville will get a recording contract."

I never did find out if that young man ever made it in the music business or not, because I was too busy trying to fix our old bus to learn his name. There is whole lot more to a music career than standing on stage and singing to the crowd.

Sometime after that Merle wrote a song titled, "Shade Tree (Fix-it Man)" that we put on *Swinging Doors*, our third album. The lyrics to the first part of the song are:

> *Well I am a shade tree fix it man*
> *I don't need a helping hand*
> *I am a jack of all trades*
> *When I am working in the shade*
> *I am a shade tree fix it man*
>
> *I headed out west from Arkansas*
> *My hoopie ran fine for awhile*
> *Then the rods started knockin'*
> *The gauges started rockin'*
> *She wouldn't run another mile*

Sometimes being a shade tree fix-it man can help you get down the road to your next show. I never asked Merle who he had in mind on that song, but I am from Arkansas, so who knows, maybe I was the one.

We always had a problem with the brakes on that first bus. When it rained and there was a lot of water on the road, the brakes would not work properly so we had to be very careful. One rainy day we were traveling on a two-lane road in the mountains of East Tennessee when we topped a hill to discover that a car was at the bottom of the hill, stopped in the road to make a left-hand turn. Dean Roe Holloway, Merle's childhood friend and bus driver for many years, hit the brakes to stop, but they failed. He could see that the car was a station wagon filled with children. So, Dean turned the bus off the road and into the ditch. We had a rough landing, and when we stopped, the bus was almost on its side. Fortunately, he missed the car full of children, and the bus was not badly damaged. We got a tow truck to pull us out and were able to continue on our way.

As I look back on that rainy day, I now realize that God was surely watching over us. I felt the same way that day that I did in my truck in Korea, when the mortar fire stopped just before it reached me. Years later, Merle wrote a song called "Mama's Prayers" about the protective hand of God in his life. In one line in the song Merle wrote, *I felt a mighty hand* as he described another near bus wreck. Well, I felt a "Mighty Hand" that day, and God surely protected that family and us on that hill in Tennessee.

After Merle's career began to take off, we decided to buy a new bus. We were able to upgrade and get a much better ride for the road. We took the old bus and painted it, and made it look really good. We had originally paid forty-five hundred dollars for that bus. Buck Owens was interested in it, because he wanted to use it as a remote radio station for his radio station, KUZZ. So, we sold the bus to Buck for six thousand dollars. That was a great price for that old bus, and I am still proud of that deal after all these years.

CHAPTER 12

Glen Campbell's First Big Hit

MERLE ALWAYS SAID THAT GLEN Campbell had more God-given talent than any person he ever met. We used Glen on numerous recordings on our early Capitol sessions. Back then he was an A-list studio musician, and one of the top guitar players in the business. Glen played on hit records for Frank Sinatra, Elvis Presley, The Beach Boys, and just about everyone else in the 1960s. He fit right in with our band because he loved country music, and he was a good ole boy from Arkansas—just like me. We all knew Glen was going to be a star someday.

Glen played guitar and sang harmony vocals on several of Merle's biggest hits. You can hear him on "Swinging Doors," I'm a Lonesome Fugitive," "Sing Me Back Home," "Branded Man," "Mama Tried," and many other songs. He made a huge contribution to our early recordings, and he helped create the sound that made Merle Haggard a country legend. When you put Merle Haggard,

Bonnie Owens, and Glen Campbell in the studio singing on a recording, you couldn't help but have a hit.

"Mama Tried" is considered by many to be Merle's greatest song, and it has received numerous awards. In fact, just before Merle passed away, we learned that "Mama Tried" was placed into the National Recording Registry of songs at the Library of Congress in Washington, DC. A song receives that honor if it has made a significant impact on American history and culture. "Mama Tried" was also selected for the Grammy Hall of Fame in 1999.

When we recorded "Mama Tried" in 1968, we used Glen Campbell, James Burton, and Roy Nichols all on guitar. In my opinion, these were the three best guitar players in the world at that time. Glen also sang harmony with Bonnie. When you listen to the studio version of "Mama Tried," you are not just hearing Merle Haggard, you are also listening to Glen Campbell.

Norm Hamlet likes to tell people that he only played two notes on "Mama Tried." Those who listen carefully to the song will notice a distinctive two note beat that concludes the introduction. Norm and Roy called this the "Batman" lick, because the two notes sounded similar to the last two notes from the *Batman* television theme song. Those two Batman notes are also heard at the very end of the song. Norm takes a great deal of pride in those two notes at the beginning and the end of "Mama Tried."

The chorus to "Mama Tried" contains one of the most familiar lines in all of country music. When Merle sang this song in his concerts, the audience usually sang right along with him. From a songwriter's perspective, I have always been fascinated by the phrasing in the chorus of this song. Merle used the words "Mama tried" three times in a row, yet somehow it fit perfectly:

> *I turned twenty-one in prison doing*
> *life without parole*
> *No one could steer me right*
> *but Mama tried, Mama tried*
>
> *Mama tried to raise me better*
> *but her pleading I denied*
> *That leaves only me to blame*
> *'cause Mama tried*

In 1967, Glen was helping us in the studio when he asked Merle and the band if we wanted to listen to the latest song he had recorded. He then played, "By the Time I Get to Phoenix" on the big speakers at the Capitol Records' studio. We were all impressed by the song and felt it was going to be a hit. Back in those days, we sent out demo singles to radio stations all over America, and asked disc jockeys to play our songs. That was one of the ways we promoted our music. If the disc jockeys played a song and gave it airtime, then the artist was on his or her way to having a hit.

Merle told Glen that we were going to send "By the Time I Get to Phoenix" out with his next demo to all the radio stations, and that he would place a note in each demo asking the disc jockeys to play Glen's song. So, Glen brought two thousand copies of "By the Time I Get to

Phoenix" to Bakersfield, and we packaged them together and sent them out—with Merle's note inside—all over the country. We got our office staff, my family, and Merle's family, and we all stuffed those records into the packages. Glen's song soared to the top of the charts, became one of the greatest love songs of all time, and Glen became a country music superstar.

We had arranged for Glen to be our opening act on our next tour, but this was before his big hit made it to the top of the charts. Merle told Glen that we would release him from his obligation to us so he could go on the road on his own. Glen certainly could have made a lot more money doing that instead of being our opening act, but he chose to go with us on the tour. Glen and Merle had great respect for one another, and no one appreciated Merle Haggard more than Glen Campbell.

CHAPTER 13

Okie from Muskogee

MERLE WROTE COUNTLESS SONGS GOING down the high-way, and that is understandable because we spent nearly half of our lives on a bus. Once, as we were driving on Interstate 40 in Oklahoma, Merle saw the exit sign for Muskogee. His family had migrated to Bakersfield from a farm near Muskogee in the 1930s.

Lillian Rea, Merle's sister, tells the story that their barn burned down on the farm in Oklahoma, and their father made the decision to move to California. All the rest of Merle's family had been born in Oklahoma, but he was born in California. I guess you can say that Merle was a California Okie.

Norm Hamlet remembers the first time Merle showed the band the song, "Okie from Muskogee." He was still trying to work out the words for the second verse, and could not remember what the sandals were called that the hippies were wearing at that time.

Eddie Burris, our drummer said, "They're called roman sandals."

Merle responded, "Okay, I'll make you a co-writer on the song, and you'll get a percentage of the royalty."

Today, Eddie's name is still listed as co-writer of "Okie from Muskogee," but he only wrote two words, "roman sandals." Merle did this with several people in the band over the years. He might give someone like our bus driver, Dean Holloway, or Bonnie, credit for helping him with a line in a song, and then give them part of the royalty. Merle could be generous to a fault. The verse in the song, "Okie from Muskogee" that Eddie Burris got credit for writing is:

Leather boots are still in style
for manly footwear
Beads and roman sandals
won't be seen

Merle asked what I thought about the song. I told him I was concerned, because I had never heard the words marijuana or LSD used in a country song. I was afraid disc jockeys might not play it because many of them smoked marijuana, and they might not like the message that was being communicated. However, I felt if they gave the song airplay, it would be a hit.

My fears about the song were unfounded, because disc jockeys back in 1969 did not hesitate to play it. In fact, I learned that the hippies loved it, too. Jerry Garcia and the Grateful Dead, and The Beach Boys were soon playing

"Okie from Muskogee" in their concerts. Everywhere we played it, the crowd sang right along with Merle and the band, and it became one of Merle's biggest hits. The opening line: *We don't smoke marijuana in Muskogee*, is one of the most familiar lines in all of country music. Most people who don't know anything about country music or Merle Haggard do know this song.

Everywhere we played "Okie from Muskogee," the audience went wild. Merle loved the crowds' reaction, and he wanted to make a live recording of it on our next tour. He hoped to try to capture the enthusiasm of the crowd on an album. When I got home, I drove to Hollywood and purchased everything we might possibly need to make a live recording. We placed all of the equipment into a rented work van, and created a mobile studio. Our goal was to record every concert on our next tour that was scheduled for Texas and Oklahoma. We wanted to record a couple of songs at each location, and put the whole thing together in a live album.

We took off on our next tour with the recording van following along. We started in Texas and began to record every concert, but never got anything we could use. Something went wrong at every show. For example, at a show in Texas, they had a rotating stage that no one told me about. We were getting a great recording when the promoter began to slowly rotate the stage so the crowd could see better. As the stage began to move, it unplugged every cord I had, so that ended that recording. Something like that happened at every concert, and we had nothing to show for all the hard work and money we had put into the project.

Our last concert date for the tour, though, was in Musko-gee, Oklahoma, so we had one more chance to get the concert and the song recorded live.

Lewis Talley and I worked feverishly to get the equipment set up for the recording in Muskogee, and it took a long time to get everything in place. The time for the concert was fast approaching, and Merle kept asking, "Fuzzy, are we going to make it?" We were just minutes away from starting the show when we finally got everything finished. We recorded the entire concert without one problem, and when you listen to the album, *Okie from Muskogee (Live in Muskogee, Oklahoma)*, you can hear what we got on the recording on that magical night. The crowd was packed into that auditorium in Muskogee, and when Merle began to sing "Okie from Muskogee," I thought they were going to tear the place down. I do not think I have ever heard a louder crowd anywhere.

The performance, the crowd, and the recording came out perfectly. We had been so disappointed in trying to get a recording at the other concert locations, but now we had what we needed. The album was not to going be live from several different locations, but just live from Muskogee. We were able to record one of the most iconic recordings in country music history, and it could not have been in a better location than Muskogee, Oklahoma.

I brought the recording home to Bakersfield, and began to edit it down. Ken Nelson at Capitol had no idea what we had done, and when I took the recording to Los Angeles and showed him what we had, he was not happy. He could not believe that I made the recording without consulting him about it. However, when he listened to it, he changed his thinking.

We continued to edit the recording in Los Angeles and soon released it. Capitol had already sent out a studio version of "Okie from Muskogee," but quickly requested that all of those be sent back. Capitol only wanted to sell the live album version of the song. If you have a studio single of "Okie from Muskogee," you have a rare piece of country music history. Capitol wanted the people to buy an album, not just a single.

After we released the song, we went right back out on the road. I saw Ken Nelson about a month later, and he told me that "Okie from Muskogee" had sold over two hundred fifty thousand copies in the first couple of weeks. So, all of our hard work paid off, because the song was a smash hit. Within a few months Capitol wanted to do their own live album. They brought in their engineers with their fancy equipment, and recorded *Merle Haggard Takes Philadelphia—Live!*, but it did not come close to what we had accomplished in Muskogee.

After "Okie from Muskogee" was released, things really began to change for all of us. We were booking bigger venues, and were making a lot more money. When I look back on all the trouble we had trying to record the song, and then finally getting such a great recording on our last try, I just can't help but believe that God was guiding us the entire time. Merle became a superstar country artist after that song, and he was known from then on as Merle Haggard, the Okie from Muskogee. I think it is the best recording I ever made.

CHAPTER 14

Merle's Music Was Out of this World

MERLE HAGGARD'S MUSIC WENT TO the moon. I mean literally, his music was taken to the moon by astronauts on the 1972 Apollo 16 lunar flight. Imagine my surprise when NASA contacted our office in Bakersfield to request a cassette of Merle's music. Charles Duke, one of the three astronauts on Apollo 16, was a big Merle Haggard fan and wanted to listen to Merle's music on the mission.

We were all excited to receive this request from NASA, and Merle and the band went to Buck Owens' studio on Chester Avenue in Oildale to record a personal message for the astronauts, and then placed several songs on the tape. One of the songs included on the recording was Merle's current number one hit at that time, "Daddy Frank (The Guitar Man)." Gordon Terry, our fiddle player, had told us about a traveling family band he had heard about in Florida that had a lead singer who was blind, and whose wife was deaf. Merle was inspired by the story and promptly wrote a song about them that became a number one hit.

"Daddy Frank" had become a family affair for Merle and me. The song is about a family band, so Merle suggested that we use our daughters as back-up singers on the recording. My daughters, Cindy and Robin, along with Merle's daughters, Dana and Kelli, joined Bonnie to be the family singers on the recording. The girls did such a good job that we used them on a couple of concert dates in Nevada and California. When we sang "Daddy Frank" on the stage, we brought out the girls, and they were a big hit.

Merle wrote songs like "Daddy Frank" all the time. He'd hear a story or something would happen to him and then he turned that experience into a song. No one could write a story song better than Merle. That was the case with his number one hit, "Legend of Bonnie and Clyde." Back in 1967 we heard about the new *Bonnie and Clyde* movie and went to see it. Merle was always fascinated by American outlaws, maybe because he once was an outlaw himself. He loved that movie, and saw it over and over again. Finally, he came in one day with a new song about the famed duo. Merle was captivated by Faye Dunaway, who played Bonnie in the movie. Now, I have seen the real pictures of Bonnie Barrow, and she did not look at all like Faye Dunaway.

When we were in the studio recording "Legend of Bonnie and Clyde" Glen Campbell played guitar and helped on the vocals, as usual. After we finished the song, Merle said, "Wait a minute, we need a banjo on this tune." You may remember that the theme song for the movie,

Bonnie and Clyde was "Foggy Mountain Breakdown," which was a Flatt and Scruggs song that highlighted Earl Scruggs's banjo picking. Flatt and Scruggs was always one of my favorite groups, and I loved their bluegrass music.

"Does anybody play the banjo?" Merle asked.

"I do," Glen said.

Merle suggested we find a banjo and have Glen lay down a track to see how it sounded. So, we went to a large music store near the Capitol Records' studio and found a banjo. We talked the owner into renting it to us so we could use it on the recording. When we finished, we took it back to the store. I have often thought that somewhere, someone has that banjo and they have no idea Glen Campbell played it on a number one hit song for Merle Haggard.

For the recording, Glen borrowed finger picks from Norm Hamlet, went off in the corner, and began to try to work out the song. In a short time, he came back and said, "I've got it." We recorded him playing that song, and that is how we got the banjo on "Legend of Bonnie and Clyde." However, that is not the end of the story.

The next time we used Glen in the studio he told us a story about his banjo playing. Glen was driving in Los Angeles and singer/songwriter John Hartford was in the car with him. Hartford had written the song, "Gentle on My Mind," which was another huge hit for Glen, winning three Grammy awards. Hartford was also an accomplished banjo and fiddle player, and he was a regular on Glen's television show, *The Glen Campbell Goodtime Hour*.

As they were traveling down the freeway, Merle's Bonnie and Clyde song came on the radio, so Glen reached over and turned it up, so he could hear the song. Meanwhile, John just sat there and did not say a word. So, Glen turned it up a little louder and asked John, "How do you like that banjo playing on Merle's big hit?"

Hartford replied, "That's the worst banjo playing I've ever heard."

"Well, thanks a lot," Glen said, "because that's me playing the banjo."

"I don't care, Glen, that's still the worst sounding banjo playing I've ever heard," said John.

We all got a big laugh about John Hartford's criticism of Glen's banjo playing. John Hartford may not have been impressed with the song, but country music fans were, and "Legend of Bonnie and Clyde" went to number one. Glen and Merle were two of the best in the business, and there always was magic in the studio whenever they recorded together.

Another great story song that Merle wrote was "Kern River." The storyline in that song is about a heartbroken lover who lost his girlfriend to the swift waters of the Kern River. The song is not a true story about Merle, because as far as I know, he never lost a girlfriend in the Kern. However, people who live in Bakersfield certainly know stories about someone who did lose a loved one in that river. The Kern is the fastest falling river in the lower forty-eight states. Its headwaters start northeast of Bakersfield at Mount Whitney (which is over fourteen thousand feet tall and is the tallest mountain in the contiguous United States), and flows approximately one hundred miles down to the San Joaquin Valley, right through Bakersfield.

In the early summer, the Kern River is extremely swift and dangerous, and hundreds of people have drowned in it. Merle loved the Kern River, and when he became successful, he built a huge house on it, at the mouth of the canyon, east of Bakersfield. He could walk right out his back door and be fishing in a few minutes. The story behind "Kern River" came from his experience growing up in Bakersfield. Here are the lyrics:

I'll never swim Kern River again
It was there that I met her
It was there that I lost my best friend

And now I live in the mountains
I drifted up here with the wind
And I may drown in still water
But I'll never swim Kern River again

I grew up in an oil town
But my gusher never came in,
And the river was a boundary
Where my darlin' and I use to swim

One night in the moonlight
The swiftness swept her life away
And now I live on Lake Shasta and
Lake Shasta is where I will stay

There's the South San Joaquin
Where the seeds of the dust bowl are found

And there's a place called Mount Whitney
From where the mighty Kern River comes down

Well, it's not deep nor wide
But it's a mean piece of water my friend
And I may cross on the highway
But I'll never swim Kern River again

Sometime before we wanted to record "Kern River," Merle had gotten into an argument with an executive at our record label in Nashville. After ten years with Capitol Records, we moved to MCA Records, then eventually to Epic Records. Apparently, the executive at Epic did not like the song, and said that no one had ever heard of the Kern River. I was not there, but Merle told me later that he threatened to whip the guy. I would not have messed with Merle if I had been that man, because Merle knew how to take care of himself.

Merle spent most of his youth in the juvenile court system, then spent more than two years of his life in San Quentin, so he knew how to fight—and fight dirty. Merle was not going to be intimidated by a Nashville music executive in a suit. The executive did not know what he was talking about because "Kern River" climbed into the top ten on the charts. Merle knew his audience, and people still love that song today.

Merle wrote a number of songs that mentioned the Kern River. One of the last songs he wrote was a Jimmy Rodgers-sounding tune titled, "Kern River Blues." Rodgers was a legendary country, blues, and folk singer-songwriter who passed away back in 1933. Merle's song is about Bakersfield, Oildale, and the Kern River, which separates the two towns. The people and places in Merle's life often found their way into his songs.

Merle and I both loved to fish, and we spent many happy hours fishing our favorite spots on the Kern River. On one of those fishing trips up the river, we ran into our good friend and fellow musician, Red Simpson. Red was a singer/songwriter best known for his trucking songs. He soon began to tell us quite a fish story. He claimed that the day before he had caught a five-pound fish right where we were fishing.

Merle said, "I'll pay you five hundred dollars for that fish."

"Well Merle," Red said, "I wish I could throw up and give him to you, because I ate him last night."

We had recorded several of Red's songs through the years, including one on our very first album. Red had several hit records, including a big hit on a song called "Highway Patrol."

We also took our fishing gear with us on the road. In the early days we had a difficult time booking Monday through Wednesday shows, so we had plenty of time to fish. Later, we could book a concert on any night of the week, but that success did cut back on our fishing.

Our kids were all great friends and they grew up together, fishing and swimming almost every summer. My youngest daughter, Robin, and Merle were very close, and they had a unique bond. He loved to reminder her that he had once saved her life. When Robin was ten years old, she mis-stepped on Merle's dock on Lake Shasta, and she and the little dog she was walking both fell into the water.

Robin could swim, but with the surprise of the fall and the little dog thrashing about, she began to struggle in the water. Merle was the closest one to her, so he reached in and pulled her to safety while the dog swam to shore. Merle reminded her of that the last time they were together in Bakersfield, not long before he passed away. Merle has always been Robin's hero. That's just one more reason why I always smile when I recall that our little family band sang on the song "Daddy Frank," and the Apollo astronauts took it to the moon.

CHAPTER 15

Bob Wills, Merle's Favorite Bandleader

MERLE AND THE STRANGERS ALL loved Bob Wills' music, and his Western swing sound. For those of us living in California in the years after World War II, we were able to see and hear Bob Wills on a regular basis. He played in Bakersfield on many occasions, and his music was always on the radio. Before he came to California, Bob was based out of Tulsa, Oklahoma, and every Saturday night his show was broadcast live from Cain's Ballroom in Tulsa. After the war, Bob followed his audience to the central valley in California to play music for all the people from Oklahoma, Texas, Arkansas, and Missouri who had migrated west.

Bob Wills created a sound that took country music instruments, and mixed them with big band instruments to make a unique hybrid sound that he called Western swing. He always traveled with a large band that included a piano player, numerous fiddle players, a steel guitar player, a horn section, and a large vocal group.

I actually played with Bob Wills and his band on one occasion. My band was playing at Oakwoods Park in Kingsburg, California, near Fresno, and Bob Wills and the Texas Playboys were on the same bill that afternoon. His steel player had way too much to drink the night before, and could not perform. So, Bob's bandleader asked if I could sit in with the band for the show. During one tune, Bob looked at me and nodded for me to take the next instrumental break, so I jumped right into the part. Bob came and stood right next to me as I was playing, and gave his signature "Ah-Ha" call right in the middle of my solo. I will never forget that moment!

All through the show, an older fellow in the crowd called out something to Bob between songs. Bob was patient and said, "We will get to that in a minute," but I never could understand what the man was actually saying. Finally, when we played "San Antonio Rose," the man hollered out in excitement with a speech impediment and said, "Hot d . . n, Sam Amtonio Wose!" That was what he wanted to hear, all along. I like to think I was one of Bob's Texas Playboys—at least I was for one show.

Several years later, Spade Cooley was in Bakersfield, and I was asked to play steel in a house band at the famous Maison Jaussaud restaurant, where he was playing. Spade Cooley was another Oklahoman who came west, and made it good in the music business. He played for years in Santa Monica, and is often credited with being the "King of Western Swing." This is a step up from David Stogner's designation as King of West Coast Western Swing. No one really knows who started Western swing, but I did get to play with both Bob Wills and Spade Cooley. Sadly, Spade Cooley's life ended in tragedy, because in 1961, he was convicted and sent to prison for murdering his second wife, Ella Mae Evans. His famous trial was held right here in Bakersfield.

During his lengthy music career, Merle recorded four tribute albums to his favorite artists. These albums were dedicated to Jimmy Rodgers, Bob Wills, Lefty Frizzell, and Elvis Presley. Merle loved Bob Wills music so much that he set out to learn the fiddle, just like Bob. Merle worked and worked on the fiddle, and in time became a really good player. I can still remember him walking back and forth on the bus, practicing. He drove us all crazy learning to play that thing on the road. Merle always kept Bob Wills' music on the bus, and he absolutely loved Tommy Duncan's singing. Tommy was a founding member of the Texas Playboys, and recorded and toured with Bob Wills on and off into the early 1960s. Merle never grew tired of listening to Bob's music.

Merle always wanted to put together a big band, like Bob Wills had, and when he became really successful, that is exactly what we did. We were fortunate that many members of Bob's band were still alive and playing music. We were able to hire Tiny Moore, Eldon Shamblin, Joe Holley, Alex Brashers, Jim Belkin, Johnny Gimble, and others from the Bob Wills Texas Playboys band. Merle loved to conduct the band on stage, just as Bob Wills had, and he used his fiddle bow to direct the music as he imitated Bob's mannerisms. Merle even perfected the famous Bob Wills "Ah-Ha" when the musicians played.

In 1970, we brought the Strangers, and a number of band members from the Texas Playboys into the studio to record the Bob Wills tribute album. Sadly, Bob suffered a stroke just before we started the project. Norm Hamlet remembered that the Strangers had to practice and get ready to play the songs that were going to be recorded. The Strangers were all familiar with the tunes, but had not played them in a long time. Norm anticipated that when they got to the studio with the Texas Playboys, that they would go over the songs a couple of times to make sure everyone was ready, but it did not happen that way. Merle asked the Playboys how they wanted to play the songs, and one of them said, "Merle, you just count off the song, and we'll be ready." So, that is what Merle did. Merle counted off the song and those Texas Playboys were fabulous.

Everybody had a great time playing Bob's music, and the album climbed all the way to number two on the charts. Everyone from the Strangers was thrilled to play with these legends of Western swing, and with that album, Merle was able to introduce a whole new generation of country music fans to Bob Wills and the Texas Playboys.

After Bob Wills suffered a stroke, he fell on hard times. A promoter asked us to play at a Bob Wills benefit concert in Texas, and we were happy to do so. I remember Merle specifically instructed me to make sure that our pay for the show got to Bob. When we got the check, I took it and personally gave it to him. There were more than a few crooked promoters in the music business, and Merle wanted to make sure that Bob was not cheated. Merle was very generous to his family and fans, but he never wanted anybody to know anything about it, so I will say no more.

CHAPTER 16

Bonnie's Favorite Merle Haggard Song

MANY OF MERLE'S BEST SONGS came from personal experiences, and I believe that was true of his biggest song, "Today I Started Loving You Again," which was on Merle's 1968 Bonnie and Clyde album.

The story behind the song is one of my favorites. We were in Fort Worth, Texas on a long road trip, and the band and crew were staying in two different hotels right across the road from one another. We had a night off, and I was anxious to get a good night's rest. I had just gotten settled into bed when Merle called. "Can you come over to our room and listen to this new song? Bonnie has just written it down."

Merle often wrote songs like that. He sang them, and she wrote down the words. Bonnie always kept a pen and paper nearby, because she never knew when Merle might come up with a new song. Bonnie was a good songwriter in her own right, and she often contributed words, phrases, and ideas to his songs. In fact, she is listed as a co-writer on "Today I Started Loving You Again."

When Merle called that night, I had to get out of bed, put on my clothes, and walk across a busy road to get to their room. When I got there, he began to sing me the new song. Then he asked what I thought of it, and I said, "Merle, it is a hit!" And it was. That song has been recorded by more artists than any other song Merle ever wrote, and to date it is his best money maker. Millions of people have heard Merle Haggard sing "Today I Started Loving You Again," but that night in a hotel room in Texas, I was the first person to ever hear it performed.

We recorded the song at the Capitol Studios in Hollywood. I actually played bass guitar on the recording while our usual bass player sang harmony with Bonnie. I am not a bass player by trade, however I did play bass on hits for Buck Owens, Tommy Collins, and of course, Merle. Our original plan was to arrange this love song as we did on "Sing a Sad Song," with big orchestration and strings, but that was not what happened.

First, we laid down the rhythm section of bass, acoustic guitar, and drums with the vocals. Then Merle said, "Let's listen on the big studio speakers and see what we have." When we played it back, everyone was in agreement that the song did not need anything else. I am so glad that we did not add big orchestration and strings to that track.

Merle has been called the "Poet of the Common Man" and the lyrics to "Today I Started Loving You Again" is the perfect example for that title:

Today I started loving you again
I'm right back where I've really always been
I got over you just long enough to let my heartache mend
Then today I started loving you again

What a fool I was to think I could get by
With only these few million tears I've cried
I should have known the worst was yet to come
And that crying time for me had just begun

'Cause today I started loving you again
I'm right back where I've really always been
I got over you just long enough to let my heartache mend
then today I started loving you again

Capitol placed "Today I Started Loving You Again" as the B side of the single, "Legend of Bonnie and Clyde." Their thinking was that Bonnie and Clyde was going to be a bigger hit, because of the success of the popular movie at that time. Sure enough, the Bonnie and Clyde song went to number one, and "Today I Started Loving You Again" only made it to number five. The fact is, all these years later few people remember "Legend of Bonnie and Clyde," but his song, "Today I Started Loving You Again" is still being sung and recorded around the world.

Those who listen carefully to the song will notice the reverb on Merle and Bonnie's vocals. The recording studio at Capitol records had the best echo chambers in the world. The Capitol building is an iconic, round building in Hollywood that looks like a stack of LP records. The basement of the building is also round, and it is divided into several pie shaped echo chambers. When we wanted reverb on a song, we played the recording through a speaker in the echo chamber, and then positioned a microphone in the room to capture the natural reverb.

There was one particular echo chamber in the basement at the studio that we thought was the best, and we used it on "Today I Started Loving You Again." I know that today reverb is created digitally for a song, but my experience was that nothing can beat the real thing that we got in those echo chambers. I also believe that Merle wrote "Today I Started Loving You Again" with Bonnie in mind. She always said it was her favorite Merle Haggard song, and I can understand why, because Merle almost certainly wrote the song for her.

Merle Haggard and Buck Owens, both Bakersfield artists, both hit the big time. But the powers that be in Nashville seemed to have a problem with that. For more than a decade, music that came out of Bakersfield dominated the charts. Together, Merle and Buck produced almost sixty number one hits between 1965 and 1975. They also had an innumerable list of top ten songs.

Country music legend George Jones once told me that there was a lot of jealousy in Nashville over the success that was happening in Bakersfield in those days. And, country superstar Vince Gill has said that the golden age of country music was in the 1960s and 1970s, and that the golden music came out of Bakersfield, not Nashville. I have no doubt that both were right.

Merle did move to Nashville at one point and stayed for several months, but he quickly returned to Bakersfield. Everyone told him he had to be based out of Nashville to make it. Later, he said that the time he spent in Nashville was the most unproductive time of his entire career.

There was a difference in the music coming out of Nashville and Bakersfield, and Nashville had a hard time accepting it. For example, Merle's band, the Strangers, received the country music band of the year award nine times from the West Coast-based ACM awards show.

During that same time period, even with all of those number one hits, the Strangers never once received the Nashville-based Country Music Association (CMA) award. They were nominated, but in the end were always overlooked.

Life on the road is tough, and can be especially difficult on a marriage. Bonnie and Merle had been married for more than ten years when their marriage came to an end. I was unaware that they were having serious problems when they divorced, especially as I never saw them fight or be cross with one another. I had been surprised by their marriage, and then I was also surprised by their divorce. Bonnie and Merle remained good friends after their break up, and she continued to tour with the Strangers until she was diagnosed with Alzheimer's disease.

Bonnie began to have a tough time with simple tasks as her memory began to fail. My wife Phyllis was Bonnie's best friend, and she arranged for her to be placed in a memory care center in Bakersfield. Phyllis took great care of everything for Bonnie. She took her to the doctor, cleaned her clothes each week, took her to get her hair fixed, and we both took her out to eat on a regular basis. Phyllis was also right by her bedside when she passed away.

Merle came to the memory care center to visit Bonnie and performed a small concert for the folks in the facility. Even though Bonnie had lost much of her memory, she could still remember most of the words to Merle's songs. She sang along with Merle in their last concert together at the memory care center. When the event was over, Bonnie took Merle to visit her room. She pointed to a large poster of Merle on the wall and said, "this is my favorite singer," not realizing she was speaking to Merle. It was so sad to watch Bonnie slowly slip away from all of us.

Chapter 17

Merle Haggard and the American Dream

WHILE I CONTINUED AS MERLE'S manager until the day he died, I only did recording and studio work with Merle and the Strangers until 1980 because, just after my fiftieth birthday, I began to notice that I was having trouble with my hearing. In just a short period of time, I lost my ability to hear in one ear, and only had partial hearing in the other. Today, I cannot hear a thing without my hearing aids. Because of this hearing loss, I was unable to play the steel guitar or mix a record. Fortunately, my role with Merle had evolved into much more than being a recording engineer or musician. The business responsibilities of the operation were taking more and more of my time. These duties included overseeing the booking, managing all the employees, setting up recording sessions, traveling on each road trip, and taking care of all the finances.

Sometimes I am asked if I regret giving up my musical career to work with Merle. The answer is no. My career in music still would have ended when I began to lose my hearing. If you cannot hear, you cannot play or sing. I truly believe God was directing my path when Merle and I were connected, because I was able to stay in the music business, just on the business side.

Merle Haggard really did live the American dream. He was born to parents who migrated to California from Oklahoma during the depression and dust bowl era. When he was a young man, he got in trouble with the law, and spent more than two years in San Quentin State Prison. Then he started a music career, and became the greatest country artist in history. That is not just my opinion, it is a fact that can be supported by research. (See Appendix B.) Also, it wasn't just country fans who loved Merle's music; people in every genre of music appreciated his songs. On one occasion, we received a call at our office from a promoter for the rock band, the Rolling Stones. He wanted to know if Merle could open for the Stones on a couple of concert dates. When we looked at the calendar, we realized that only one date would work, and that was a concert in Little Rock, Arkansas.

I could not help but see the irony in this concert location. My home town of Squirrel Hill, Arkansas was just a few miles north of Little Rock. I could have never dreamed that when I started my country music career as a teenager back in Arkansas, that I would ever be a part of a rock concert with one of the biggest bands of all time. When we booked the date, there were some who questioned how we would be received by a rock crowd, but I knew that, in Arkansas, Merle was bigger than the Stones.

The concert venue was packed. I walked with Merle to the stage, and watched the concert from behind a set of curtains. To my amazement, every member of the Rolling Stones, including Mick Jagger, stood just off stage so the crowd could not see them, and listened to the entire concert. Later that evening, one of the Rolling Stones managers told me he had never seen them do that. He told me the band always stayed in their dressing rooms while the opening act played, but that night, they watched the entire concert like all the other fans in Little Rock.

After the show, the Rolling Stones hosted a party. They wanted to meet us, and have their picture taken with Merle. We visited and talked about music late into the night. It was easy to see that the Rolling Stones were huge Merle Haggard fans. I will never forget seeing all the equipment that traveled with the Stones. I went out into the parking lot and counted twenty-one huge semi-trucks and trailers that they used for their concert tours. At that time, no one in country music traveled like that.

Bob Eubanks was our booking agent in the 1970s and he became one of our closest working partners through those years. Bob later went on to host *The Newlywed Game* and other TV game shows, but his role back then was to book our shows and get us a bigger payday, if possible. Bob's family was from Missouri, and he grew up a country music fan. A lot of people do not realize that Bob was also a real rodeo cowboy, and won several awards for his calf roping skills. Bob is still a good friend to this day.

Bob started out as a disc jockey in Los Angeles, but soon became a promoter for rock 'n' roll acts. His career really took off when he booked the Beatles into the Hollywood Bowl in 1964. Now, if you can promote the Beatles, you probably can handle just about anyone. Bob booked us all over the world, including England, Australia, Ireland, Canada, Alaska, and just about everywhere else you can imagine. Bob was able to book us in places I could never have dreamed of us playing, and he helped take Merle's career to another level.

One of the most important dates he ever booked for us was the White House in 1973. The convicted felon, the Okie from Muskogee, was going to play for President Nixon and his wife in the East Room of the White House. The year before, in 1972, Ronald Reagan (who was then Governor of California), had granted Merle a complete pardon of his criminal record. So, Merle was able to clear a background check to meet the president.

The concert date was on Saint Patrick's Day, which was also Mrs. Nixon's birthday. Merle wrote a poem for Mrs. Nixon to honor the occasion, and presented it to her at the concert. Flossie Haggard, Merle's mother, also accompanied us on that historic trip to the White House. The opening act for Merle's show that night was the bluegrass band, The Osborne Brothers. All of Nixon's staff, people such as Henry Kissinger, Bob Haldeman, John Ehrlichman, and many others really seemed to enjoy the show. I especially remember the great reaction they gave Merle and the band when they played "Okie from Muskogee." The news about the Watergate burglaries had just come out, and in a little over a year, Nixon would have to resign.

Following the concert, the president invited everyone in the band and crew to a reception where we all got to shake hands with the president and Mrs. Nixon. They gave us a tour of the White House, and even opened up their private residence. Merle had come all the way from 1303 Yosemite Drive in Oildale, California to 1600 Pennsylvania Avenue in Washington, DC. For those of us who were fortunate to be at the White House with Merle, it was a night we will never forget.

We also played for President Ronald Reagan when he was in office. He invited us to play an outdoor concert at what was called the Western White House, at his famous Rancho Del Cielo home in the mountains above Santa Barbara, California. When we arrived at the ranch, we were welcomed by the first lady, Nancy Reagan. At that time, early in the afternoon, the president had not yet arrived. We began to set up and get everything ready for the concert when we heard a helicopter approach. As it got closer, we saw it was Marine One, the presidential helicopter. It was impressive to see the president land in his helicopter at the ranch, and we had a great concert for about two hundred people including the president, the First Lady, and the White House staff. After the concert we all got a chance to meet President Reagan and the many guests who had been invited.

In July 2007, Kern County renamed a three-and-a-half-mile stretch of 7th Standard Road in Bakersfield, Merle Haggard Drive. Anyone who drives south on Highway 99, and first enters the outskirts of Bakersfield, will intersect with Merle Haggard Drive. The road is actually located in a suburb of Bakersfield known as Oildale, which was Merle's hometown. One mile east of Highway 99 on Merle Haggard Drive, is Meadows Field, Bakersfield's airport. A brand new commercial center is currently being built on Merle Haggard Drive at the airport called the Silver Wings Commercial Center, in honor of one of Merle's big hits. That way, those who drive through Bakersfield, or fly in or out of town at the Bakersfield airport, will be reminded of Merle Haggard and his music.

Merle was born April 6, 1937 at the Kern County General Hospital in Bakersfield. Many people have been told that Merle was born in a railroad train boxcar, but that is just not true. He was born in a hospital, but did grow up in a small house in Oildale that was a converted railroad boxcar.

His dad was a carpenter who worked for the railroad, and Mr. Haggard remodeled the old boxcar and converted it into a house. He had the boxcar moved to a lot at 1303 Yosemite Drive in Oildale, and turned it into a very comfortable home for his wife and son, Merle. Later, he added on a bedroom and built a screened-in full, sized-porch onto the front. Flossie Haggard was very fond of the house, and said it was her favorite home in which she ever lived. The little house was perfectly insulated because it was a refrigerated boxcar, so it was cool in the summer and warm in the winter.

The story is often told that poor Merle was born into abject poverty, and that his mother had nowhere to deliver him, but in an abandoned railroad boxcar. Well, that is just legend, and not true. It was a small, cozy, cute little house built by Merle's father. The entire family is very proud of it, and some of Merle's children remember staying there with their Grandmother Haggard when they were little. I visited Mrs. Haggard in her boxcar home countless times. Just across the street from the boxcar is the church that Flossie Haggard attended every Sunday, and it's the church where Merle was baptized as a ten-year-old boy.

The cozy little house was located just a few feet from a short railroad spur that ran between an oil refinery, and the main line of the north and south railroad tracks were a couple miles west of Merle's home. The house was close enough to the tracks that it rumbled and rattled the boxcar when the train passed by every day. When Merle was a child, the train was pulled by steam engines. You can really appreciate the opening line in Merle's huge hit "Mama Tried" when the real story about the location of the boxcar home is understood. That opening line is:

The first thing I remember knowing
Was a lonesome whistle blowing

The line to that song is true, and some of Merle's first memories were hearing those steam trains with their steam whistles pulling the oil tanker cars from the refinery to the main line. He always remembered the sound of the steam whistle blowing as it passed by their little home. Merle loved trains. I think they always reminded him of his dad, whom he loved dearly and missed to his dying day.

Merle wrote a number of songs about his life as a child growing up in Oildale. One song that really expresses the memories of his happy childhood days with his mom and dad living in the boxcar is the song "Oil Tanker Train." This tune was never a big hit for Merle, and we placed it on his 2010 album, *I Am What I Am*. The lyrics describe life in the boxcar when Merle was a child, before his dad passed away.

The oil tanker train from down on the river
In Southern Pacific and Santa Fe names
Would rumble and rattle the old boxcar we lived in
And I was a kid then, and I loved that old train

Loaded with crude oil, headed for town
The boxcar would tremble from the top to the ground
And my mother could feel it even before it came
"Get up," run to the window, here comes the oil train

From my checkered past I can always bring back
The memories we felt in that home by the track
And all these years later, it's still stuck in my brain
Oh, I loved that old oil tanker train

Dad worked for the railroad when I was a kid
And my favorite memories were things that he did
Early one Christmas after Santa Claus came
There next to the tree ran a toy tanker train

From my checkered past I can always bring back
The memories we felt in that home by the track

And all these years later, it's still stuck in my brain
Oh, I loved that old oil tanker train

The last trip Merle made to Bakersfield was in July of 2015 when the boxcar was moved from its location in Oildale to the Kern County Museum's Pioneer Village. A huge caravan met at the home site, and followed the big semi tractor-trailer loaded with the boxcar to the museum where it has now been completely restored and placed on public display.

Kern County Sheriff Donny Youngblood provided an escort for the truck that carried the boxcar, and for Merle's bus, and all of the people who followed along. The boxcar parade passed by Standard Elementary where Merle attended grade school as a child. Then the long line of cars continued on Chester Avenue, past Buck Owen's Oildale studios where many of our songs were recorded. Finally, we crossed the Kern River and came to the museum.

Over the years, Merle and Sheriff Youngblood had become good friends. There was an irony to their relationship, because many years before, Merle was running from the Kern County Sheriff's Office, and now they met him at the county line to provide him a sheriff's escort to his old home.

We had a nice ceremony at the museum that day, and afterward, Merle left the old boxcar. To my knowledge, never saw it again. He wrote a song that expressed some of the emotion that he experienced that hot July morning, though, and as far as I know, "Kern River Blues" was the last song Merle wrote and sang himself. He passed away less than a year later. The words to this Jimmy Rodgers-style blues song are:

I'm leaving town tomorrow
Get my breakfast in the sky
Well, I'm leaving in the early morning

Eating breakfast in the sky
Be a donut on a paper
Drink my coffee on the fly

I'm flying out on a jet plane
Gonna leave this town behind
I'm flying out on a jet plane
Gonna leave this town behind
They've done moved the city limits
Out by the county line

Put my head up to the window
Watch the city fade away
Put my head up to the window
Watch Oildale fade away
The blues back in the thirties
Are just like the blues today

There used to be a river here
Running deep and wide
Well they used to have Kern River
Running deep and wide

Then somebody stole the water
Another politician lied

When you closed down all the honky-tonks
The city died at night
When you closed down all the honky-tonks
The city died at night
When it hurts somebody's feelings
Well a wrong ain't never right

Well I'm leaving town forever
Kiss an old boxcar goodbye
Well I'm leaving town forever

Kiss an old boxcar goodbye
I dumped all my blues in the river
But the old Kern River's dry

I cannot think of anyone whose life experience was like that of Merle's. He was in solitary confinement in prison when he was twenty years old, and then just a few years later, he was playing music for the President of the United States at the White House. If that is not the American Dream, I don't know what is.

Long before the height of his career it was apparent that Merle could do it all. He could sing a song, play a song, and of course, write a song. He is best known for his singing and songwriting abilities, but Merle Haggard was also a great guitar player—and he became an excellent fiddle player. He constantly worked on his craft as a musician.

And, virtually everything he wrote from 1965 to 1975 went to number one, or made it into the top ten in the charts.

Merle's tenth studio album, *A Portrait of Merle Haggard*, was released in 1969 and contained the songs, "Working Man Blues," "Silver Wings," and "Hungry Eyes." He received four BMI (Broadcast Music Incorporated) awards that year. BMI has been around since the 1920s, and recognizes songwriters for their hit songs, giving awards for nine different genres of music each year. I follow the music industry very closely, and while it may have happened, I cannot remember a songwriter who received four BMI awards in a single year.

During his career, Merle received over sixty BMI awards. He had so many of them that he had to store them in a loft in a barn on his property. He also received the BMI Icon Award, which is given to songwriters to honor their "unique and indelible influence on generations of music makers." In the country genre, the Icon Award has only been given to songwriters Bob DiPiero and Dean Dillon; producer Billy Sherrill; artists Mac Davis, Vince Gill, Kris Kristofferson, Hank Williams Jr, Willie Nelsen, Charlie Daniels, Loretta Lynn, Dolly Parton, Bill Anderson; and of course, Merle Haggard.

CHAPTER 18

It Hurt Me in an Old Familiar Way

IN MY EARLY DAYS IN country music, I enjoyed some success as a songwriter. However, when Merle really began to write songs, I realized very quickly that I was not in his league. The first time Merle played the song "Hungry Eyes" for me, I said, "Merle, that's it. I am going to quit writing songs!" Who can keep up with that kind of talent? Merle knew God had given him an incredible gift. Lillian Rea, Merle's sister, loves to tell a story about Merle when he was an infant. She always reminded us that their father was a good musician, so music was in his DNA. When Merle was an infant and the family was living in the boxcar, Mrs. Haggard showed Lillian how Merle responded to country music on the radio. Whenever she placed Merle close to the music, Merle began to tap his feet together in perfect time to the song. Mrs. Haggard pointed this out to Lillian, and said, "Look, he has music in him, just like his dad."

No one could keep up with Merle's songwriting ability. When I told him that I was going to quit writing, he said, "Fuzzy, you taught me how to put a country song together." That is high praise from one of America's greatest songwriters. Merle was being kind when he told me that, because he has to be mentioned along with Hank Williams as one of the best songwriters of all time. Songwriting is what kept him at the top of the music business for over fifty years. Merle could really write a song . . . and I tried.

In 1959, I gave Ray Price a song I had written titled "Same Old Me," which was a love song about a lonely man who is hoping his girl will come back to him. The song reached number one on the country charts and was my second number one hit after "Dear John Letter." The opening line to this song reads:

When I saw you with your new love today
It hurt me in an old familiar way

Merle took the second line from that song, *it hurt me in an old familiar way* and used it in "(Tonight the) Bottle Let Me Down." We both liked having a key phrase in a song that stood out and became memorable. That phrase must have been memorable to Merle, because he placed it in his third big hit. When I wrote a song, I always tried to describe what people were experiencing in their own lives. In "Same Old Me" I tried to connect with folks who had the heartache of waiting for someone to notice them. "Same Old Me" was a good song for both Ray Price and me. The lyrics go:

When I saw you with your new love today
It hurt me in an old familiar way
And I know there is nothing I can do
You will always find me waiting here for you

With the same two arms still missing you
And the same old heart still being true
And the same two lips that still belong to you
And the same old me keeps loving you

I have tried everything to drive you from my heart
But the memory of you makes me feel so blue
And with every heartbeat I can feel the teardrops start
So you'll always find me waiting here for you

With the same two arms still missing you
And the same old heart still being true
And the same two lips that still belong to you
And the same old me keeps loving you

Ray Price was one of country music's biggest stars in the late 1950s, and no one could have sung it better than the "Cherokee Cowboy."

Rose Maddox had a top ten hit with a song I wrote titled "Kissing My Pillow." Rose was a huge country star in California, and was on Capitol Records with us. Before her solo career, she was part of the famous Maddox Brothers and Rose band. For years, they were one of the hottest country acts on the West Coast, and played in Bakersfield all the time. Their music was a mix of old-time country and rockabilly. No act could put on a better show than Maddox Brothers and Rose. Their band was one of the first to wear colorful Western-style costumes on stage, and they were great singers, musicians, and entertainers. You had to see them live to really appreciate them.

"Kissing My Pillow" is another sad love song about a man or woman who is heartbroken after a break up. Several different artists, both male and female, have recorded the song over the years. So, the message of the tune applies to everybody.

I tell myself I'm satisfied to live the way I do
And it was such a foolish thing to fall in love with you
I tried to make believe I'm glad you found someone new
But I can't hide the loneliness, it just keeps showing through

And I keep kissing my pillow, staring at the wall
And I keep hearing your footsteps coming through the hall
And I keep counting the million dreams that never came true
And I keep kissing my pillow and pretending it's you

I never knew how much I cared until you walked away
And left me with these memories that's in my heart today
I thought that I could find somebody else to take your place
But memories of loving you keep standing in the way

And I keep kissing my pillow, staring at the wall
And I keep hearing your footsteps coming through the hall
And I keep counting the million dreams that never came true
And I keep kissing my pillow and pretending it's you

"Same Old Me" and "Kissing My Pillow" have the same basic structure with two verses, and the chorus repeated twice. This simple formula for a country song also fits the time frame for a recording that I hoped to get played on the radio. Merle and I often talked about this kind of word crafting, and how a song should be put together. We both agreed that if a song was to become memorable, it must be kept simple.

Merle became the master of this, and it is one reason why so many people remember the words to his songs. Consider "Today I Started Loving You Again," which is a very simple song with only one verse, and the chorus repeated twice. The wording to a good country song should allow the listener time to hear the story that is being told. If the simplicity of the words can be matched to the melody, then you will have a good country song.

In 1959, I gave acclaimed songwriter Harlan Howard a verse and a chorus to a song that I was working on titled "One You Slip Around With." He finished the tune, and his wife Jan recorded it. I was surprised to hear the song on the radio a little over a week after I gave it to Harlan. He obviously finished it quickly, and got Jan into the studio. The song climbed to number fifteen on the charts and it was Jan Howard's first big hit. Harlan Howard lived in Los Angeles in those days, but later moved to Nashville. He wrote songs for Buck Owens, Johnny Cash, and countless others.

Harlan is credited with the saying that country music is just "three chords and the truth." Several other artists recorded "One You Slip Around With," including Jean

Shepard, and Skeeter Davis. The big idea of the song is how lonely someone feels when his or her spouse cheats:

I had the key to heaven when we married
And for a while I brought you happiness
But now your love for me is dead and buried
And every night you share another's kiss

And I'd rather be the one you slip around with
Than be the one whose dream of love is gone
Yes, I'd rather be the one you spend your time with
Than be the one at home left all alone

Deep down inside I know that I should leave you
How many tears must fall before I learn
I think of many ways that I could grieve you
And yet I'm always here when you return

But I'd rather be the one you slip around with
Than be the one whose dream of love is gone
Yes, I'd rather be the one you spend your time with
Than be the one at home all alone

The title for the song, "One You Slip Around With," is a bit misleading. At first it sounds like a cheating song, however, when you listen to the story in the song, it is about the loneliness of the person who has been wronged. Some of the biggest country hits ever recorded have been sad songs. All three of the above songs, "Same Old Me," "Kissing My Pillow," and "One You Slip Around With," are sad country songs. Everyone who knows me knows I am not a sad person, but I did discover that sad songs do sell.

Bonnie and Merle's duet album, *Just Between the Two of Us*, was a big hit in 1966. As mentioned earlier, we recorded three of my songs on that album, "Slowly but Surely," "I Want to Live Again," and "Stranger in My Arms." "Slowly but Surely" did very well here in the United States, and it reached number one on the charts in Australia. So, I like to tell people that it was another number one hit for me—at least in Australia!

Bluegrass artist, Rhonda Vincent, and country artist, Daryle Singletary recorded "Slowly but Surely" a couple of years ago. Rhonda called me to ask several questions about the song and told me it was one of her mother's all-time favorite Merle and Bonnie songs. I recently heard bluegrass singers Kenny and Amanda Smith's recording of the song, and they also did a fine job on it. We recorded that song over fifty years ago, and it is still going strong:

> *Slowly but surely I'm falling in love*
> *Falling in love with you*
> *Slowly but surely you're winning my heart*
> *And you're winning my heart too*
>
> *Slowly but surely I'm losing my heart*
> *And I'm losing my heart to you*
> *Slowly but surely, my dreams will come true*
> *If I spend my lifetime with you*

You're just what I wanted
You're just what I needed
You're my every dream come true

My loves growing stronger
I can't wait much longer
I'm falling in love with you

Slowly but surely I'm falling in love
Yes, I'm falling in love
Falling in love with you

Slowly but surely I'm losing my heart
And I'm losing my heart to you
Slowly but surely, my dreams will come true
If I spend my lifetime with you

You're just what I wanted
You're just what I needed
You're my every dream come true

Most of my songs were love songs. I never really could write about pickup trucks, trains, or drinking. I was thrilled when "Slowly but Surely" was a number one hit in Australia, all the way on the other side of the world, and am also thrilled today that it is still being sung in the Appalachian Mountains by bluegrass bands. You just never know how long a song might last, or how far it might go.

I also wrote several novelty songs in my early days of songwriting. These songs were very popular in the 1950s and early 1960s, and many of them became smash hits. I always hoped I could cash in on one of these big hits, but none of mine ever did much.

Bakersfield's Dallas Frazier's first big hit as a song-writer was a novelty song titled "Alley Oop," about a character in a comic strip. Dallas wrote several big hits for Merle, but his first song on the charts was a silly one. Gary Paxton produced and recorded the tune, and it was sung by his group, The Hollywood Argyles. Paxton was based in Bakersfield for a while, and released several country hits on his Bakersfield International label. He also produced the big novelty hit, "Monster Mash." Both of these songs reached number one on the pop charts, and made lots of money.

"Ole What's Her Name" (recorded by Wynn Stewart in 1967) was by far the best of my novelty tunes. Merle used to sing that song in our early concert dates, and The Malpass Brothers are still singing it today.

One of my earliest attempts at writing a novelty song was "Arkie's Got Her Shoes On." As kids growing up in Arkansas, we hardly ever wore shoes, and most of the women walked around the house barefoot. When ladies put their shoes on and went to town, that was a big deal. So, I wrote the following song:

> *Arkie was a bashful girl*
> *She never went nowhere*
> *And everybody laughed*
> *Because her feet were always bare*

But then when she grew older
She began to notice things
She bought herself a pair of shoes
My how that girl changed

Arkie's got her shoes on
She done come uptown
Arkie's got her shoes on
She going all around

She found herself a boyfriend
She tired of staying home
Everybody watches cause
Arkie's got her shoes on

She is looking at the bright lights
While going on her way
She had never been to town before
At least that's what they say

The boys all follow her around
They won't leave her alone
Everybody watches cause
Arkie's got her shoes on

Arkie's got her shoes on
She having lots of fun
She always has got a great big smile
For each and everyone

Everyone is happy
 When she comes around
She brings you joy, and boy oh boy
She will never let you down

I recorded this song on the Tally label and distributed it locally in Bakersfield. Later, it was placed on a the first of a two-volume compilation album, *The Other Side of Bakersfield 1950s & 60s, Vol 1: Boppers and Rockers from Nashville West.* The album set also includes songs by Billy Mize, Tommy Duncan, Buck Owens, Bill Woods, Tommy Collins, Hillbilly Barton, Ferlin Husky, The Farmer Boys, Johnny Bond and Dallas Frazier. That is pretty good company. This album set is made up of songs that are considered to be rockabilly or early country/rock songs that came out of Bakersfield. The album also contains a song that I recorded on Tally records written by Buck Owens titled, "Yer fer Me!" I never thought of these songs as rockabilly, or as rock 'n' roll tunes. In my mind, we were just having fun playing country music in Bakersfield.

I wrote one novelty song that I never recorded called "Take My Love and Jam Up Your Heart." No one has ever heard of it, and probably for good reason. Here is the first verse:

You don't like the way I part my hair
I tried so many ways to make you care
But you bring me down before I even start
So take my love and jam up your heart

"Ole What's Her Name." "Arkie's Got Her Shoes On," and "Take My Love and Jam Up Your Heart" never won a Grammy or BMI award, but they were a lot of fun to write and sing.

I am just turning ninety years old, and am still trying to write songs. A songwriter can't help but write. The older I get, the more I remember the times long ago, including those days when I was in the army on the front lines in Korea. I recently started a new song as I was thinking about what the people of Korea faced during that war. The name of the song is "The Pusan Blues." Pusan (now known as Busan) was a city at the southern end of the Korean Peninsula where many of our American soldiers were stationed. When I witnessed the suffering of those people in that war-torn country, it left a lasting impression on me. The first part of the song says:

> *As you look up and down the roadside*
> *Pappa San is all dressed in white*
> *Momma San with a dozen children*
> *Is coming down the road in fright*

> *You ask them where they come from*
> *Back up the road a mile or two*
> *They saw the rice paddies doing the "burp gun boogie"*
> *So, they've got the Pusan Blues*

I am sure many people in Korea still have the "Pusan Blues." I know that I never can, or will, forget the people there.

CHAPTER 19

A Big Night in Washington, DC

OVER THE COURSE OF HIS career, Merle Haggard received virtually every award the music industry had to offer. He was eventually placed into the Country Music Hall of Fame, and the Songwriters Hall of Fame in Nashville, Tennessee. He also received numerous Grammy and BMI awards, and was named entertainer of the year at both the CMA and ACM awards. In December of 2010, Merle received the most prestigious award of his career when he was given the Kennedy Center Honor. This annual award is given to individuals in the performing arts for their lifelong contribution to American culture. The ceremony takes place each December at the John F. Kennedy Center for the Performing Arts in our nation's capital.

When Merle was notified that he was going to receive this honor, it set in motion quite an operation. He was allowed just a limited number of family and friends who could attend the event with him. My wife, Phyllis, and I were fortunate to be part of Merle's party that night. He brought his wife, Theresa, a few of his children, his nephew Jim Haggard, and our bus driver Ray McDonald. Merle, Theresa, and my wife all flew, and met us in Washington. Jim, Ray, and I drove the bus all the way across the country from California to attend the big ceremony.

Merle received the Kennedy Center Honor award, along with Paul McCartney of the Beatles, Oprah Winfrey of movie and television fame, music composer Jerry Herman, and dancer and choreographic director Bill T. Jones. Following the ceremony, the Kennedy Center hosted a reception and we got to meet and have our pictures made with all of the honorees. Oprah asked me to take a picture of her with Paul McCartney. I did my best, but I am no photographer. I have always wondered if that picture was any good. If not, Oprah will never forgive me, because that was probably her one and only time to have her photograph made with Paul McCartney. I also was able to have my picture made with the former Beatle, and he seemed like a real nice fellow. Merle and Paul McCartney are perhaps the two best songwriters of my lifetime, and it is remarkable to consider just how many hits those two men have written. I guess it doesn't get much bigger than Merle Haggard and the Beatles!

Only eight country artists—Roy Acuff, Willie Nelson, Dolly Parton, Johnny Cash, George Jones, Loretta Lynn, Reba McEntire, and of course, Merle Haggard—have ever received the prestigious Kennedy Center honor. When we were in Washington, an official with the Kennedy Center told us that the honor was similar to receiving knighthood from the Queen of England. That award solidified Merle's place in American culture as one of the most significant country artists of all time.

During the ceremony, they honored the accomplishments of each artist. The tribute to Merle began with a video narrated by Vince Gill to honor Merle and his music. Vince said that Merle was his "life-long favorite," then he and Brad Paisley sang and played a rousing rendition of Merle's big hit, "Working Man Blues." Everyone was rocking at the Kennedy Center during the guitar solos by those two amazing players. Vince and Brad did a fantastic job on the song, but I still believe you can never beat what James Burton did on the original recording back at Capitol Studios in 1969. His guitar solo on "Working Man Blues" is one of the most imitated guitar solos ever recorded. Every country guitar player tries to learn the licks that James Burton played on that record. No disrespect to Vince and Brad, but James Burton set the bar pretty high.

Miranda Lambert and Kris Kristofferson sang "Silver Wings," and Willie Nelson and Sheryl Crow sang Merle and Bonnie's big hit, "Today, I Started Loving You Again." Then, to end the tribute, Willie Nelson, Jamey Johnson, and Kid Rock sang "Ramblin' Fever." On the last chorus, Vince Gill, Brad Paisley, Miranda Lambert, and Sheryl Crow all came back out on stage, and they finished the song together.

When they played Merle's music that night at the Kennedy Center, I was amazed at how the crowd reacted to his songs. The house was full of politicians, celebrities, and other dignitaries and they all seemed to be big Merle

Haggard fans. I reflected back on the days when we worked up those tunes, and took them into the studio to record. I realized that night that Merle's music had touched the world. Later that evening we met President Barack Obama and former President Bill Clinton at the reception that followed the awards ceremony. Throughout my career in music I met Richard Nixon, Ronald Reagan, Bill Clinton, and Barack Obama. Back when I was a barefoot boy in Squirrel Hill, Arkansas, a boy who just wanted to play the steel guitar, I could never have imagined that I would meet four United States presidents.

In spite of the accolades that Merle received that night, he never got a big head. He was ready after the ceremony to get back out on the road and start playing music again. Soon, we were pulling the bus into a Denny's to get some breakfast, and head out to the next concert. As one of his songs says, *he's been a working man dang near all of his life*.

Over the years, we met almost every major celebrity in the music, television, and the political world that anyone could imagine, yet none of them seemed to impress Merle very much. He preferred the company of those who were with him from the start of his career, and he kept all the Bakersfield boys around him throughout his life. He obviously was one of the greatest singers, songwriters, and artists of all time, but to us, he was just another guy from Bakersfield who liked to play country music.

CHAPTER 20

The Bakersfield Players

MERLE WROTE A LINE IN his song "Beer Can Hill" that sums up how he felt about his hometown of Bakersfield:

Well, you could do better
but you won't do bad in Bakersfield

All of us in the music business from Bakersfield feel the same way, because Bakersfield proved to be the right place for a new country sound to emerge. Maybe we could have done better somewhere else, but we didn't do bad right here in Bakersfield.

In the 1950s and 1960s, there was plenty of great country music talent living in California, and we were able to draw upon those talented musicians and songwriters to help create the Merle Haggard sound. I have heard Bakersfield called Nashville West, but out here we like to say that Nashville is Bakersfield East.

It's amazing to consider how many musicians, singers, and songwriters came out of Bakersfield during those days. Gerald Haslam, author of W*orkin' Man Blues: Country Music in California* (with Richard Chon and Alexandra Haslam), once stated that in the 1960s Bakersfield had two hundred musicians, thirty-five songwriters, ten music publishing companies, five studios, three recording labels, and two booking agencies.

Merle was by far the biggest talent to come out of Bakersfield, but he readily acknowledged that his success was a team effort. Ray McDonald, Merle's bus driver, remembered seeing Merle get emotional the last year of his life, when he talked about his Bakersfield team that worked for him throughout his career. Several of these Bakersfield musicians, singers, and songwriters made major contributions to Merle's music.

Norm Hamlet was the leader of Merle's band for more than forty years. I do not know of another musician/bandleader who worked for the same artist for that length of time. Norm probably holds the record for that kind of job.

He was born in Farmersville, California, which is located in Tulare County, just east of Visalia in the San Joaquin Valley. His family was originally from Arkansas, but they relocated to Antlers, Oklahoma during the 1930s. In time, they migrated to California, so I guess Norm is both an Arkie and an Okie. He for sure is a "prune picker." If your parents migrated to California from Oklahoma, Arkansas, Texas, or Missouri and then you were born out here, you are called a "prune picker" by the locals.

Norm replaced me on the steel guitar when I became Merle's personal manager and started to work full time on the business side of the operation. Norm began his music career playing for a very popular group in the 1950s called The Farmer Boys. Like Norm, they were from Farmersville, California, and that's where they got the name for their band. Bobby Adamson and Woodie Wayne Murray made up the act, and their families had migrated to California from Arkansas, just like so many of us in California's central valley had. The Farmer Boys had a couple of hit songs and also toured with some big acts in the late 1950s, including Elvis Presley.

Norm was playing with The Farmer Boys at the County Line Club between Lancaster and Rosamond, California when he met the Mandrell family. The family patriarch, Irby Mandrell, approached Norm one night in the club, and asked if he would give steel guitar lessons to his young daughter. They worked out a simple agreement where Norm would stay in a spare bedroom at the Mandrell home on the weekends when he was playing at the club. Then, each week he could give steel guitar lessons to Irby's young daughter, Barbara. According to Norm, the steel guitar came easy for her, and she learned quickly. Of course, Barbara Mandrell went on to become a country music superstar.

Several years later, Norm recommended that we hire Barbara's sister, Louise, to play with our band. Louise became one of the few female Strangers, and like her sisters, was an excellent musician and singer. Today, when you visit Norm at his home, you will find a glass case in his entry hall that contains numerous awards that he and the Strangers won over the years. One plaque that he has on display is a set of Barbara Mandrell's first steel guitar finger picks. She gave them to Norm many years ago, as a thank you for being her steel guitar teacher. So, Norm is not only a great steel guitar player, he is also a really good teacher.

Norm joined the Strangers in 1967 and played on every album following that. He also made every tour with us until Merle passed away, and no one knows Merle's music better than he does. Norm is like a cook in the kitchen; he knows how those songs were prepared and presented. We could always count on Norm to provide a great stage performance, and he was an excellent studio musician. Studio work is a high-pressure job, because a musician needs to get the song right the first time, if he can, and Norm could do that. He not only played steel guitar for us, he also played the Dobro on a number of Merle's songs.

A great example of Norm's Dobro playing can be heard on a Dallas Frazier song that we recorded in 1976 titled "California Cotton Fields." He and Roy Nichols always worked well together and their styles complemented each other. Norm never tried to be flashy with his playing, and he always wanted to provide the right support and proper accent to Merle's voice. I often noticed when the band was playing on stage that Norm had his hands in his lap, not playing a note. He knew a musician did not have to play every single note of a song for the band to have the right sound. He has great timing and taste, and continues to play a busy schedule with Merle's sons Noel and Ben.

Norm remembers countless details about how we recorded Merle's biggest hits in the studio. One of his favorite stories is how we got the rhythmic percussive ringing note on "Working Man Blues." On that song's opening guitar solo by James Burton, there is a metallic sounding ring that continues throughout the entire tune. Someone in the band suggested the song needed the sound of a hammer striking an anvil as a part of the rhythm section, because this was the working man's song.

Well, there was no hammer or anvil lying around the Capitol studio in Hollywood, but Norm remembered they found a large metal stand that held a big, glass ashtray. The drummer took the ashtray, and struck it with his drumstick to produce the percussive ringing sound, just like a hammer makes when it hits an anvil. It sounded great, so we put it on the song. The Strangers' drummer may just be the only studio musician in history to be paid union scale for playing an ashtray on a number one country hit.

Many of the legendary songs that Merle wrote begin with Roy Nichol's unique guitar solos that are just as memorable, in some cases, as the words themselves. Roy played for The Farmer Boys, Maddox Brothers and Rose, Lefty Frizzell, and Wynn Stewart before he went to work for Merle. Roy and Merle had become great friends in Bakersfield, and Roy encouraged Wynn Stewart to hire Merle when their band needed to replace the bass player. Going to work for Wynn was a major step forward in Merle's music career. In time, we were able to hire Roy away from Wynn's band, and he worked for us the rest of his career. I know that when Roy left Wynn Stewart and joined our band, that he took a significant cut in pay, but Roy wanted to play with Merle. Roy Nichols played lead guitar for the Strangers for twenty-two years.

Roy never wanted to draw attention to himself on stage—or anywhere else. When we worked together on the Cousin Herb show, Roy never wanted to take a lead guitar solo. We had to force him to step into the spotlight. When Roy worked for Rose Maddox, she tried to help him understand that a musician needed to play and perform if he ever hoped to make a living in the business. She told me that when Roy was a teenager, onstage, he often sat with his back to the audience. She had a difficult time getting him to turn around and face the crowd. Most of the time in our concerts, Roy sat next to Norm, and the crowd hardly noticed him until he played one of his signature solos. He might have suffered from stage fright, but he could sure play that Fender Telecaster guitar.

Gene Moles was another Bakersfield guitar player who we used quite often in our early days of recording. I used Gene a number of times on Bonnie's records on the Tally label, and he also played on Merle's first studio album with Capitol. He was another Oklahoma guitar player who helped create the Bakersfield Sound. Gene did all of the guitar work on Red Simpson's truck songs, and also played on his big hit, "The Highway Patrol."

Gene teamed up with guitar-maker Semie Moseley, and helped build the very popular Mosrite Guitar that was built in Bakersfield. Gene was a very versatile player who worked with future Rock and Roll Hall of Fame member Nokie Edwards, of The Ventures fame, and who wrote many of the memorable surf rock instrumentals that were so popular in the 1960s. Gene could play everything from country to rock.

In the 1980s, Eugene Moles, Jr., Gene Moles' son, toured with us for several weeks, filling in for an ailing Roy Nichols. He was a great guitar player, just like his dad.

Tommy Collins was an important Bakersfield musician and songwriter who was very close to Merle and me. Tommy's real name was Leonard Sipes, and he became one of the first country singers to make it big from Bakersfield. He was a tremendous help to both of us when we first started out in the music business. I played bass on all of Tommy's 1950s hit recordings, and that studio work allowed me to meet Ken Nelson at Capitol Records, who eventually signed Merle.

Tommy was a solid musician and singer, but is best known for his songwriting. We recorded twenty of Tommy's songs over the years, and that is more than any other songwriter, with the exception of Merle himself. Two of Tommy's biggest hits for us were "Roots of My Raising" and "Carolyn," both of which went to number one. Tommy paved the way for all of the Bakersfield country artists who eventually recorded at Capitol.

In the 1960s, Tommy left the country music business to become a Baptist preacher. He left Bakersfield to attend seminary at the peak of his popularity. Pastor Tommy Collins performed the ceremony when Merle married his last wife, Theresa Ann Lane, at Lake Shasta. Tommy pastored several churches, but eventually returned to writing songs for us, and for other country singers such as George

Strait. He was certainly one of Bakersfield's best songwriters, and one of my good friends.

In 1980 Tommy wrote and recorded a song about Merle, which mentioned Bonnie and me titled "Hello Hag." In response, Merle turned around and wrote a song about Tommy titled "Leonard," which was Tommy's real first name. The song became a top ten hit, and expressed how much Merle appreciated Tommy Collins and all of the other Bakersfield musicians and songwriters who helped us in the music business. The words to Leonard are:

> *When Leonard finally came to California*
> *He was twenty-one years old as I recall*
> *He loved to write a song and pick the guitar*
> *And he came to hang a gold one on the wall*
>
> *The town in which he lived is not important*
> *But you'll know the town I mean by the time I'm through*
> *He soon became a famous entertainer*
> *But Leonard was a name he never used*
>
> *He was on his way to having what he wanted*
> *Just about as close as one could be*
> *Hey, once he even followed Elvis Presley*
> *And he wrote a lot of songs for me*
>
> *But he laid it all aside to follow Jesus*
> *For years he chose to let his music go*
> *But preaching wasn't really meant for Leonard*
> *But how in the hell was Leonard supposed to know*

Well life began to twist its way around him
And I wondered how he carried such a load,
He came back again to try his luck in music
And lost his wife and family on the road

After that he seemed to bog down even deeper
And I saw what booze and pills could really do
And I wondered if I'd ever see him sober
But I forgot about a friend that Leonard knew

Well Leonard gave me lots of inspiration
He helped teach me how to write a country song
And he brought around a bag of groceries
Hey, back before Muskogee came along

Really, I'm not trying to hide his real name
Or the town in which this episode began
Somehow I had to write a song for Ol' Tommy
If just to see the smiles in the band

Well when Leonard finally came to California
He was twenty-one years old as I recall
And he loved to write a song and pick the guitar
And he came to hang a gold one on the wall

All of the musicians, singers and songwriters were very close to one another in Bakersfield, and we all appreciated Tommy Collins.

Red Simpson was yet another musician and songwriter from Bakersfield who wrote a number of songs for

Merle. I first met Red when he was only seventeen years old, and I helped him get a job at the Clover Club—while he was still underage. He reminded me of my early days when I worked at a similar Bakersfield bar, the Sad Sack, when I was an underage musician.

Red became a trusted friend to both Merle and me, and was always willing to help us any way that he could. He was an amazing musician who could play guitar, piano, banjo, fiddle, mandolin, and steel guitar, and is best known for his trucking songs, many of which became big hits. Red also wrote a number of songs for Buck Owens including "Sam's Place," which went number one and was co-written by Buck. Red co-wrote "You Don't Have Very Far to Go" with Merle, which we placed on our first studio album in 1965. Merle also recorded Red's song, "Lucky Old Colorado," which is an absolutely beautiful song. In 1972, Merle recorded a tribute song that Red wrote called "Bill Woods from Bakersfield."

Bill gave Buck his first job at the Blackboard, and had a great eye for talent. Bill also helped numerous other country singers get their start. Merle wanted to record this song to let people know how important Bill was to the Bakersfield country music story. Merle always tried to recognize those who had helped and influenced him along the way. Red's tribute song to Bill Woods of Bakersfield says:

> *Let me tell you all a story 'bout a guitar picker man*
> *To me he is the greatest picker in the land*
> *He's taught me how to play in G*
> *And he taught me how to sing in key*

Bill Woods from Bakersfield, the Bakersfield guitar man
Well, Bill gave old Buck the first job he ever had
Bill must've been a good teacher 'cause old Buck didn't do bad
He sets up there chewin' his old cigar playin'
Wildwood Flower *on his guitar*
Bill Woods from Bakersfield, the Bakersfield guitar man

Well, Bill never hit big, but he didn't miss it far
And in my book he'll always be considered a star
I followed him and he taught me
Guitar pickin' and harmony
Bill Woods from Bakersfield, the Bakersfield guitar man

When the roll is called up yonder
*   and we must all meet our quest*
I bet he'll be chosen to pick there with the best
Up there with his gold guitar
When things get right, Bill will be a star
Bill Woods from Bakersfield, the Bakersfield guitar man

Red Simpson and Bill Woods are both gone now, but their influence on Merle's career lives on in the music they all made together.

I first met Dallas Frazier when he was a young teenage singer on the Cousin Herb show. He became one of the most significant songwriters to come out of Bakersfield, along with Merle Haggard, Buck Owens, and Tommy Collins. He wrote huge hits, such as "There Goes My Everything" for Jack Greene, "Elvira" for the Oak Ridge Boys, and "Fourteen Carat Mind" for Gene Watson.

Just about everyone has recorded a Dallas Frazier song, including Elvis Presley, Diana Ross, and Engelbert Humperdinck.

Dallas Frazier was born in Spiro, Oklahoma and migrated to Bakersfield in the early 1940s. His family were farm laborers who had a very tough go of it. Ferlin Husky spotted the talented young singer at a music contest and invited him to live with his family, so that he could help him get started in the music business.

Not long after that, another Oklahoma transplant named Tommy Collins moved in with the Husky family, and became a roommate with Dallas. Tommy had traveled to Bakersfield from Oklahoma City with his girlfriend, Wanda Jackson, who became a rockabilly star. When Wanda's family returned to Oklahoma, Tommy decided to stay in Bakersfield to see if he could get into the country music business. Ferlin also had a great eye for talent because both Dallas Frazier and Tommy Collins became two of country music's most successful songwriters.

Ferlin helped Dallas get a contract at Capitol Records in the 1950s, and the musicians on the Cousin Herb show, including me, did the studio work on his recordings. In 1954, Dallas recorded and released a single that I wrote, "I'm Gonna Move Over Yonder." He was a teenage sensation on the Bakersfield country music television shows, but his greatest talent proved to be his songwriting ability. George Jones and Connie Smith both recorded complete albums of Dallas Frazier songs.

Merle recorded Dallas' song, "California Cotton Fields" on our album *Someday We'll Look Back*. That album also contained the song "Carolyn," written by Tommy Collins, which went number one on the country charts. So, two former Bakersfield roommates, Dallas Frazier and Tommy Collins, made a major contribution to one of Merle's albums when he was at the peak of his success. "California Cotton Fields" describes the struggles of the Okie migrant trying to make a living as a farm laborer. Both Dallas and Merle could easily identify with these farm laborers, because their families migrated to California from Oklahoma.

Merle's sister, Lillian Rea remembers the hardships the Haggard family faced when they first came to California in the 1930s. She tells the story that on the first Sunday they attended church in Bakersfield, a lady asked her father where he was from, and her dad replied, "Oklahoma." The woman responded, "Well, I have heard that people from Oklahoma who have moved out here will not work." Lillian said that her dad stood up tall and said, "I never heard of an Okie who wouldn't!"

Those Okies and Arkies did work hard in the fields, and many of those same Okies and Arkies became very successful playing country music.

The album *Someday We'll Look Back* contained three songs about hard-working farm laborers. "Tulare Dust" is one of these songs, written by Merle, and is an ode to the Okie migrant who worked in the California cotton fields, just like Dallas Frazier's parents. Tulare County is just north of Kern County in California's fertile San Joaquin Valley. At one time, there were thousands and thousands of acres of cotton in the Valley. Before the day of modern and mechanized farm equipment, the cotton had to be harvested by hand, and that was hard, dirty work for the migrant farm laborer. "Tulare Dust" described life in those cotton patches:

Tulare dust in a farm boy's nose
Wondering where the freight train goes
Standin' in the field by the railroad track
Cursin' the strap on my cotton sack

I can see Mom and Dad with shoulders low
Both of them pickin' on a double row
They do it for a living because they must
That's life like it is in the Tulare dust

The California sun was something new
That winter we arrived in '42
And I still remember how my dad cussed
The tumbleweeds in the Tulare dust

The Valley fever was a common fate
To the farm workers here in the Golden State
And I miss Oklahoma, but I'll stay if I must
And help make a livin' in the Tulare dust

The Tulare dust in a farm boy's nose
Wondering when the freight train goes
Standing in the field by the railroad track
Cursin' this strap on my cotton sack

I have always been amazed how many songwriters came out of Bakersfield in the 1960s and 1970s. There must have been more great songwriters per capita in Bakersfield, California during those days than any other city in the country.

CHAPTER 21

The Strangers

NORM HAMLET WAS THE ONLY official bandleader the Strangers ever had. Before he went to work for us 1967, both Merle and I handled the band together, but when Merle's career took off we had to divide up the responsibilities, because no one person could handle it all. As previously mentioned, I took over the business side of Merle's career, and in time, Norm took over the role of bandleader for the Strangers. That allowed Merle the opportunity to concentrate on his music, and continue to give his full attention to songwriting.

Norm was perfect for the job. He was reliable and always kept the band on the stage and ready to play. The Strangers were so good that we always used them in the recording studio. We did use other studio musicians, like Glen Campbell, Ralph Mooney, and James Burton, but by and large, what you hear on Merle's recordings is our band, especially in the early years. The Strangers won nine

ACM Band of the Year awards, and most of these band members lived in Bakersfield.

Musicians are not always easy to work with, and they can make life on the road a challenge. For the most part, we were lucky to have good people, but we did have our problems with some band members. We caught some guys stealing money, and other lied or had addiction problems that we just could not tolerate. It did not happen often, but Norm did have to fire some musicians. Others, like Biff Adam on drums, Don Markham on horns, Roy Nichols on guitar, and Ronnie Reno on guitar and vocals, stayed with us for years.

Merle Haggard's career developed into quite an organization, and dozens of people were on the payroll. We had lots of income, but we also had lots out go as well. One of the reasons Merle kept working almost to his dying day was because so many people depended upon these jobs. We were all grateful that Merle liked to work, and he kept playing on the road right up until he died. Several of these people deserve special notice, because they were so close to Merle.

My cousin Lewis Tally was one of Merle's best friends, and from the beginning, he believed that Merle would be a star. Merle gave his youngest son, Benny, the middle name of Lewis in honor of Lewis Tally. Once Merle's career really got going, Merle hired Lewis to be his personal assistant, and he did whatever was needed. He drove the bus, played guitar, and helped in the recording studio. Merle described Lewis as "the most eccentric, indescribable human being I have known." When you travel to more than one hundred shows a year, and then spend time working in the studio together, it helps to have people around that you like. Lewis helped Merle and the band stay loose, and he made life on the road a little more fun and enjoyable. Lewis traveled with us until he passed away in 1986.

Merle trusted Lewis to take care of personal jobs that needed special attention. For example, Merle and Bonnie had a little dog named Tuffy that they dearly loved. Tuffy went with us everywhere, and the band and the crew loved the dog. One day Tuffy disappeared from the bus, and all of us searched for him. Sadly, we discovered that he had been run over in the parking lot and killed. Merle and Bonnie were broken hearted. Merle asked Lewis to take Tuffy back home and have him buried near the house. Lewis took care of little Tuffy, and when we got home from the tour, there was a small grave with a gravestone with Tuff's name on it placed by the pond at Merle's home east of Bakersfield. I know that was a big comfort for Bonnie and Merle

Both Merle and Bonnie loved their little dogs, and after Tuffy died Bonnie got another one that she named Away-we. This little guy loved to go on the road with us and was always so excited when we left out on tour. Bonnie always said "Away we go!" as the bus pulled away from home. So, she named her new little dog Away-we." I remember on one concert tour we had to stop the bus for a couple of hours on the road and wait so Away-we could have puppies. She gave birth to two little ones on Merle's bus.

Dean Roe Holloway was Merle's childhood friend from Oildale, and was our bus driver for many years. Merle was loyal to his long-time friends, and we were loyal to him. Dean and Merle went to grade school together in Oildale, and Dean was very close to all of Merle's family, especially Merle's mother. Merle mentioned Dean Roe in his song, "Mama's Prayers" that we placed on the album *Merle Haggard: The Bluegrass Sessions*. The song describes a night on the road when a fatal bus wreck was narrowly averted. Merle attributed that near miss to Dean Roe's driving, and his mother's prayers. The words to the song are:

> *Back when I was doing time there's a night I can't forget*
> *A mad man with a knife in hand tried to kill me while I slept*
> *But somehow the knife missed its mark*
> *   and I pinned the raging man*
> *Somehow my Mama's prayers had worked again*

> *One night while we were driving across the mighty Texas plains*
> *A car pulled out with its headlights out head-on into our lane*
> *As Dean Roe swerved and missed the car I felt a mighty hand*
> *Somehow my Mama's prayers had worked again*

> *Mama's prayers were always with me*
> *   through the battlefield of life*
> *She prayed for me and said amen in the name of Jesus Christ*

> *From the death house in San Quentin*
> *I walked away a better man*
> *Somehow my mother's prayers had worked again*

Mama's prayers were always with me
    through the battlefields of life
She prayed for me and said amen in the name of Jesus Christ

From the death house in San Quentin
I walked away a better man
Somehow my Mama's prayers had worked again

Dean is also listed as co-writer on Merle's number one hit "Big City," recorded on the Epic label in 1981. Merle gave co-writer status to several of the band members and support staff over the years. This allowed them to receive a portion of the royalties. Merle was not only loyal to his close friends, but he was also very generous. The story behind the song "Big City" is that after a two-day recording session in Los Angeles, Dean was waiting around in the bus, and was anxious to get back to Bakersfield. When Merle got on the bus after being in the studio for several hours, Dean said something to Merle about getting out of this big city with these dirty old sidewalks and going home.

Well, that's all Merle needed. He sat down and wrote "Big City," then walked back into the studio and recorded the song. "Big City" became the title track for the entire album and was another gold record for Merle. Dean's words provided the idea for the song:

I'm tired of this dirty old city
Entirely too much work and never enough play
And I'm tired of these dirty old sidewalks
Think I'll walk off my steady job today

Turn me loose, set me free
Somewhere in the middle of Montana
And give me all I've got coming to me
And keep your retirement
And your so-called social security
Big City turn me loose and set me free

Been working everyday since I was twenty
Haven't got a thing to show for anything I've done
These are folks who never work and they've got plenty
Think its time some guys like me had some fun

So turn me loose, set me free
Somewhere in the middle of Montana
And give me all I've got coming to me
And keep your retirement
And your so-called social security
Big City, turn me loose and set me free
Hey, Big City turn me loose and set me free

All Merle needed was an idea to get a song started. That day on the bus in Los Angeles he listened to his tired childhood friend, but more than likely, Merle felt the same way. Merle was a deep thinker, and always paid attention to what was going on around him.

Ray McDonald was a personal assistant to Merle for several years. He grew up in Oildale, and his best friends were Bonnie Owen's two sons, Buddy and Mike. When Merle hired Ray, he moved into one of Merle's houses at his place on Lake Shasta.

Ray viewed Merle as a father figure, and the two men shared a very unique bond. Ray is another example of how Merle kept people close to him whom he knew from Oildale and Bakersfield. Everyone wanted something from Merle, but he knew he could trust those who had been with him from the beginning. An irony of the name Strangers for his band was that we were not strangers at all to Merle. We were his best friends.

My daughter, Cindy Blackhawk, worked for Merle for several years and she described life in the office: "The last office Merle had in Bakersfield was the one on River Boulevard, on the Panorama Bluffs. I went to work there my junior year in high school as a receptionist, and it was a busy place. Bettie Azevedo was the office manager and Merle's secretary. B.J. Spence, Bonnie's niece, took care of the publishing. Jonell Montgomery, from Texas, helped with a lot of the paperwork. Several other girls came and went over the years as receptionists, etcetera, but the four of us were the constants.

"Merle, Bonnie, and my dad, Fuzzy, each had an office, and were in and out all the time. Along with the band members, there were a lot of visitors from all walks of life who dropped in for a variety of reasons. Some were fans just passing through. There was a large room in the back where equipment was stored, and where holiday parties were celebrated. The band also practiced in that room. My mom, Phyllis, often came to the office to take care of the bills. Bonnie and Mom were close friends, and Mom encouraged the entire office to dress up for Halloween, and to decorate for Christmas. It was fun.

"After I graduated from high school, I took over the royalty work full time. Bettie Azevedo was let go about then, B.J. became the office manager, and I took over as Merle's secretary. Sometime after this, the office hustle and bustle began to slow down. Bonnie, Phyllis, and Fuzzy were still in and out, but Merle was busy seeing Leona Williams in Nashville, and he wasn't in town much. When the office finally closed, B.J., Jonell, and I were the last to go."

As you can see, Merle's career required a lot of people to keep it moving forward. We needed bus drivers, office assistants, merchandise sales persons, road managers, stage hands, concession workers, booking promoters, photographers, accountants, guitar players, fiddle players, drummers, piano players, horn players, steel players, singers, bass players, recording engineers, audio technicians, sound technicians, lighting technicians and other jobs that I cannot remember. I can tell you this: it kept me busy.

CHAPTER 22

Blessed by God

I HAVE TO ADMIT THAT I was not a very religious person throughout most of my life, and often made the excuse that I was too busy for church. I did recognize that God had blessed me with my wife Phyllis, and my two daughters, Cindy and Robin. But, I now realize that God has always watched over my life. From the front lines in Korea to the countless miles of travel, crisscrossing the country with Merle and the band, He was there. My career in the music field, and especially being connected with Merle Haggard, had to be guided by a "Mighty Hand" far beyond my own ability.

After Merle died, I began to think a great deal about my relationship with God, and decided it was time for me to publicly confess my faith in the Lord Jesus Christ, and be baptized. I now attend the Valley Baptist Church in Bakersfield with my daughters. I believe it is never too late to make your peace with God.

Merle was a man of contrasts. In many ways he was like Johnny Cash or Elvis Presley. All of these artists seemingly had a dark side to them, but God's light shone through them in the end. Merle was a sinner; there is no denying it. The stories of his wild side are legendary, from his time in prison to his days on the road. His outlaw persona and honky-tonk lifestyle has been well documented by himself and others, but those close to him also saw a different side of Merle.

We knew that Merle came from God-fearing people, and that his mother was a godly woman. The influence of his mother's prayers and spiritual guidance appear in many of Merle's songs. In 1981, we released a tribute record to his mother that was an all-gospel album titled *Songs for the Mama That Tried*. Merle also recorded three other gospel albums: *Two Old Friends* with Albert E. Brumley, Jr., *Cabin in the Hills*, and *Land of Many Churches*, which was a double album.

We recorded this last album live in several churches across the country, and in the prison chapel at San Quentin State Prison, where Merle spent two and a half years of his life.

Merle had the pastor of Big Creek Baptist Church near Nashville, Tennessee deliver a brief sermon on this album. The preacher shared a clear gospel presentation that encouraged every person listening to repent and trust the Lord Jesus to be saved. Merle used his popularity as a country singer to spread the gospel on that album. Now, I'm not trying to make Merle Haggard out to be a preacher or a saint. That would be foolish, but I knew him as well as anyone, and I can tell you that he followed in the footsteps of his mother's faith.

Merle recorded many gospel songs in his career and the theme of redemption, prayer, and faith appeared in many of them, such as in "Mama Tried," which is the story of a mother's prayers for a wayward child.

There were two funerals for Merle Haggard. One was a private service for his family and friends at his home on Lake Shasta. Then, Lillian Rea, Merle's sister, held a public funeral for Merle at the Valley Baptist Church in Bakersfield.

This second service gave an opportunity for Merle's hometown to say goodbye to their favorite son. At the conclusion of that service, one of the last songs Merle ever wrote was premiered, and sung by country and bluegrass star Ronnie Reno. The title of song is "Let the Whole World Know That I Love Jesus." The words to the song are:

Let the whole world know
That we are in love with Jesus

We are all big sinners
And He saved our souls

Let the whole world know
That we've got eyes on heaven
And we're changing our streets
Back to gold

When he touches down
on the Mount of Zion
And heaven and earth
Will be made new

We're staying here
And nobody's flying
Let the whole world know
That we are repenting anew

Let the whole world know
that we are in love with Jesus
And that we are all big sinners
And He saved our souls

Let the whole world know
That we've got eyes on heaven
And we are changing our streets
Back to gold

When He touches down
On the Mount of Zion
And Heaven and Earth
Will be made new

We're staying here
And nobody's flying
Let the whole know that
We are repenting anew

Let the whole know
That we're in love with Jesus
And that we are big sinners
And He saved our souls

Let the whole world know
That we have our eyes in heaven
And we are changing our streets
Back to gold

Let the whole world know
that we are in love with Jesus
Hey we are all big sinners
And He saved our souls

Let the whole world know
That we've got our eyes on heaven
And we are changing our streets
Back to gold

Let the whole know that we are
In love with Jesus

During the last year of Merle's life our bus driver, Ray McDonald, was so good to take Merle to the doctor for his treatments for lung cancer and pneumonia. The doctor recommend surgery to treat the cancer, but Merle refused. He had surgery to remove a portion of his lung once before, and he always swore he would never have it again—and he didn't.

Ray said the doctor told Merle that he would not survive without the surgery. But, Merle told the doctor, "I am not afraid to die, because I am going home to see my dad!" as he pointed toward heaven. His dad passed away when Merle was just nine years old, and he never really got over it.

I have missed Merle every single day since he passed, but I take comfort in the fact that he is now with his dad in heaven, and I believe that I will see him again soon.

I have lived during the golden age of country music that came out of Bakersfield, California during the 1960s and 1970s. For over fifty years, I was fortunate enough to work almost every single day with Merle Haggard, the greatest country musician of all time, and my career allowed me to play and record music with some of the most talented people in county music. I left a small town in Arkansas when I was only seventeen years old and was able to travel all over the world. I have certainly enjoyed a long and wonderful career in the music business. Someone recently asked if my career with Merle turned out the way I dreamed it would. I told them, "I would not change a thing. God has truly blessed me!"

-THE END-

AFTERWORD

FUZZY OWEN WAS ALWAYS THE level head in Merle's career and was a huge reason for his success. I am so happy he is telling Merle's story, from start to end, as Merle was one of the greatest talents we will ever know. Fuzzy's words and stories will definitely tug at your heartstrings.

I always have a world of emotion flow through me when I talk about Hag. He was a true American treasure, and we will not see any like him for many years to come. Merle had the knack of making you feel like you were right there with him when he bared his heart and soul in a song. I played many shows with Merle, and together we traveled many long miles. During all that time he never lost his passion to perform, or to try to make this a better world.

Along with Bonnie Owens, Leona Williams, and Fuzzy Owen, I was often Merle's sounding board after he penned a new song. I was fortunate to have been with him in the glory days, when he set a standard for many songwriters and singers that will stand the test of time. Oddly enough, Merle always felt he had not written the best song he was capable of, or the biggest song he was yet to write. I guess that's why he was still writing right up to his death.

People always knew where they stood with Merle, and he never knew what a big star he truly was. He told me one time that he was more surprised with his success than anyone else, and that every time he had a hit record, he was humbled. Everyone loved Merle, including me, and I was so lucky to stand with him on stage, sing harmony, and play guitar. Those were some of the best years of my life.

I am so proud to have known Merle, and to have laughed and cried with him, going through the ups and downs we all face in this world. Merle has had an everlasting effect on my family, and my own musical journey. He not only was my friend, we were brothers in music and life. Rest in peace, Merle Ronald Haggard.

—Ronnie Reno

CLOSING THOUGHTS

I'VE ALWAYS BEEN A PEOPLE watcher. When I entered the world of country music, I was such a novice, but the first time I met Fuzzy Owen, I sensed that I was shaking hands with someone very special. Fuzzy was the visionary and driving force behind the Merle Haggard show, and recognized Merle's greatness before most anyone else. He believed in Merle, and produced his first recordings. From those moments forward, the two were inseparable.

Fuzzy could, and did, fill any role required in advancing Merle's life and career. He played steel guitar in the band, wrote songs for the show, produced, counseled, consoled, managed, ran sound, and drove the bus—whatever it took to get the job done.

The two of them were like brothers. Most of all, Fuzzy and Merle were loyal to each other, and Fuzzy remained steadfast from the first song all the way to the end of Merle's life. They were such a powerful duo. Throw in the Strangers and they were really something to be reckoned with! Because of Fuzzy, Merle left a lifetime of music for the world to enjoy, and generations to come have so much to glean from Merle's legacy.

I think of Fuzzy as the Yoda of the California country music scene. He is the last man standing from the original Bakersfield cast, and today, that scene revolves around his very presence. Although Fuzzy first gained notoriety as a West Coast pioneer, his contributions can never be limited to any one region. His life's works and influence on the entire story of country music are immeasurable. For anyone to get to the true heart and soul of country music, they would do well to sit at the feet of Fuzzy Owen. Above all, Fuzzy Owen is an honorable man and a gentleman whom I dearly love. I'm glad to know him and call him my friend.

—Connie Smith

APPENDIX A

Glossary of Names

I HAVE MENTIONED COUNTLESS PEOPLE in the book who were a part of Merle's life and music. Here is a quick reference to some of them.

Bill Anderson is one of Nashville's greatest songwriters. He has enjoyed a long career as a singer, songwriter, and country music television personality. "Whispering" Bill Anderson told me personally that Merle Haggard is the best singer, songwriter that he has ever heard.

Bill Woods was a Bakersfield Sound pioneer. His band, the Orange Blossom Playboys, played nightly at the Blackboard Café.

Buck Owens built an entertainment empire in Bakersfield. He recorded nineteen number one hits and helped create the Bakersfield Sound.

Bob Wills created the Western swing style of country music. He was from Turkey, Texas, and played music in Bakersfield on a regular basis.

Dallas Frazier is one of Bakersfield's best songwriters, and wrote songs for almost everyone in country music. Dallas often played on Herb Henson's television show, as well as several other country music television shows in Bakersfield.

Dean Roe Holloway was a childhood friend of Merle's, who drove our bus for years.

Don Markham was the horn player for the Strangers for forty plus years.

Ferlin Husky was one of the first country artists from Bakersfield to become a star. He sang on "Dear John Letter" along with Jean Shepherd in 1953.

Frank Mull handled all the concessions for Merle Haggard's concerts, and for decades helped as a road manager.

Harlan Howard was an influential California songwriter who co-wrote with me on "One You Slip Around With." Harlan was married to Jan Howard, and this song was her first hit record. He eventually moved to Nashville and became a country songwriting legend.

Herb Henson was a huge television country music star

in Bakersfield. I played on his daily television show, *Cousin Herb's Trading Post TV Show*, for almost ten years.

Irby Mandrell was the father of country music legend Barbara Mandrell. His daughter, Louise, played with our band, the Strangers, for a short time.

Jean Shepard was often called the first star of the Bakersfield Sound. She sang the hit, "Dear John Letter" in 1953 and moved to Nashville where she joined the Grand Ole Opry.

Jelly Sanders was a respected and much used musician on numerous country songs that came out of Bakersfield. Jelly played on countless Capitol Record recordings.

Joe Maphis was known as "The King of Strings" and was a top studio musician. His famous double neck guitar playing made him a favorite on California country music television shows. After playing at the Blackboard Café in Bakersfield, Joe and his wife, Rosa Lee, wrote the big hit, "Dim Lights, Thick Smoke, and Loud, Loud Music."

Johnny Bond played as a regular on Tex Ritter's country music television show, *Ranch Party*, and he also played with Gene Autry for many years.

Ken Nelson was the director of the country music division at Capitol Records in Los Angeles. He signed Merle to his first major recording contract.

Lefty Frizzell was a country legend who sang in Bakersfield on a regular basis. His unique style of singing greatly influenced Merle Haggard.

Liz Anderson was a successful country music singer and songwriter from Sacramento, California. She wrote several big hits for Merle, and her daughter, Lynn Anderson, also had a very successful music career.

Lewis Talley, my first cousin, was a close friend and associate of Merle's. Lewis started Tally Records, which I own today.

Maddox Brothers and Rose was billed as America's most colorful hillbilly band, and was an influential California country music band. Rose Maddox eventually had a solo career and recorded my song, "Kissing my Pillow," which was a top fifteen hit.

Norm Hamlet is a great steel guitar player, and was the band leader for the Strangers for over forty years. Norm still lives in Bakersfield and is a wonderful friend. Only three men played steel guitar for Merle Haggard. They are Ralph Mooney, Norm Hamlet, and me.

Ralph Mooney was the best steel guitar player I ever heard. He played for Wynn Stewart, Merle Haggard, and Waylon Jennings. He is a true stylist on the steel guitar.

Ray Price was called the Cherokee Cowboy, and was a giant country music singer in the 1950s and 1960s. He recorded my song "Same Old Me," in 1959 and it became a number one hit for us.

Rhonda Vincent is a bluegrass star who recently recorded my song "Slowly but Surely." Fifty years after I wrote it, that song is still a favorite in bluegrass jam sessions.

Roy Nichols was a lead guitar stylist in Merle's band. His unique sound helped create the Merle Haggard sound.

Tommy Collins was an early Bakersfield country music singer/songwriter. He wrote several hits for Merle—and many other country stars. Tommy became a Baptist preacher for a time, then returned to a career as a country music songwriter.

Tommy Duncan was the lead singer for many years in Bob Wills' Texas Playboys band. He was one of Merle's favorite singers.

Wynn Stewart was a country music star in the late 1950s and 1960s and had several hits. Merle worked in his band for some time, and Wynn allowed Merle to record his song, "Sing a Sad Song" that became our first hit.

APPENDIX B

Top Country Artist's List

IN **2014,** CMT (COUNTRY MUSIC Television), conducted a survey of one hundred country music artists, and asked them to list their top forty favorite artists from all music genres. The following is the CMT Top 40 artist choices. Notice that Merle Haggard is listed at number one.

1. Merle Haggard
2. Hank Williams
3. Elvis Presley
4. Dolly Parton
5. George Strait
6. Garth Brooks
7. Willie Nelson
8. Johnny Cash
9. Reba McEntire
10. George Jones
11. Loretta Lynn

12. Michael Jackson
13. Ray Charles
14. The Beatles
15. Patsy Cline
16. Taylor Swift
17. Bruce Springsteen
18. Bob Dylan
19. Vince Gill
20. The Rolling Stones
21. Hank Williams, Jr.
22. Tom Petty
23. Dwight Yoakam
24. James Taylor
25. Alabama
26. Stevie Wonder
27. The Eagles
28. Bob Wills
29. Brooks & Dunn
30. Conway Twitty
31. Miranda Lambert
32. Led Zeppelin
33. Emmylou Harris
34. Flatt & Scruggs
35. U2
36. Kenny Rogers
37. Charley Pride
38. Tim McGraw
39. Buck Owens
40. Aerosmith
40. Alan Jackson
40. Carrie Underwood

A list like this will certainly cause debate, and people can argue that one artist is more deserving than another. However, the list does confirm what I heard over and over again through the years. Countless country music artists told me that Merle Haggard was either their favorite singer or that he was the biggest influence on their music.

APPENDIX C

The Strangers and the Support Staff

THERE WERE A LOT OF Strangers who played for us during Merle's career, and each one contributed to Merle's success in one way or another. The following is a list of players that Norm Hamlet and I put together of all the Strangers we can remember. We may have forgotten a name or two, because so many played with us during our fifty years together, but here is the most comprehensive list of the Strangers we could come up with:

Bass Guitar
Billy Joe Clayton
Dennis Hromek
Doug Colosio
Eddie Curtis
Gene Price
Jerry Ward
Joe Reed

Kevin Williams
Leon Copeland
Mike Leach
Taras Produniak
Wayne Durham

Drums
Biff Adams
Brooks Liggatt
Bob Galardo
Eddie Burris
Helen Price
James Curtis
Jeff Angraham
Jim Christy
Johnny Barber
Tommy Ash

Guitar
Benny Haggard
Bobby Wayne
Clint Strong
Eldon Shamblin
Eugene Moles Jr.
Gene Moles
Joe Manuel
Norm Stevens
Ray Nichols
Red Volkart
Ronnie Reno

Fiddle

Gordon Terry
Jim Belkin
Johnny Gimble
Paul Anastasia
Scot Joss
Tiny Moore

Piano

Doug Colosio
Floyd Domino
George French
Mark Yeary

Horns

Don Markham
Gary Church
Renato Caranto

Singers

Bonnie Owens
Leona Williams
Louise Mandrell
Ronnie Reno

Through the years we also had many who worked for us on our support staff. These employees were critical to the success of Merle's music. They were not musicians or singers, but without them, Merle's career would not have been successful. The following is a list of our support staff:

Office Staff
Bettie Azevedo
Bob Newcomb
Cindy Owen Blackhawk
Dennis Bottomly
Frank Meadors
Frank Mull

Sound Technicians
Asa Kelly
Bob McGill
Greg McGill
John Wilson
Loren Kemper
Loren Slumbaugh
Pete Magdaleno

Bus Drivers
Dean Holloway
Fuzzy Owen
Jim Haggard
Lewis Talley
Ray McDonald

Appendix D

Fuzzy's Greatest Hits List

WHEN I TRY TO CREATE a Merle Haggard "most popular" song list, it seems like an endless task. The following is an attempt to list some of Merle's biggest hits, but this is by no means exhaustive:

All My Friends Are Going to Be Strangers
Are the Good Times Really Over?
Big City
Branded Man
California Cotton Fields
Carolyn
Daddy Frank (The Guitar Man)
Farmer's Daughter
Fightin' Side of Me
Holding Things Together
Hungry Eyes
I Always Get Lucky with You

I Take a Lot of Pride in What I Am
I'm a Lonesome Fugitive
If We Make it Through December
If We're Not Back in Love by Monday
It's Not Love but it's not Bad
Just Between the Two of Us
Kern River
Mama Tried
Movin' On
Okie from Muskogee
Prison Band
Ramblin' Fever
Roots of My Raising
Sam Hill
Silver Wings
Sing Me Back Home
Slowly but Surely
Somewhere Between You and Me
Swinging Doors
Legend of Bonnie and Clyde
Today I Started Loving You Again
(Tonight the) Bottle Let Me Down
Tulare Dust
Twinkle, Twinkle Little Star
Working Man Blues
You Don't Have Very Far to Go

I could go on and on with this list, but I believe I have made my point.

Appendix E

Bonnie Owens Songs

HERE IS A LIST OF some of Bonnie's songs that we recorded on the Tally label, and also some that we recorded on Capitol:

Consider the Children
Excuse Me for Living
Live a Little
No Tomorrow
Number One Heel
Please Don't Take Him from Me
That Little Boy of Mine
Waggin' Tongues
Why Don't Daddy Live Here Anymore?
Wonderful World
You Don't Have Far to Go

Appendix F

Fuzzy's Songs

I ALSO WROTE AND RECORDED numerous songs in the 1950s and into the 1960s. Here is a list of some of my songs:

Arkies Got Her Shoes On
Dear John Letter
I Want to Live Again
I'm Gonna Move Over Yonder
One You Slip Around With
Same Old Me
Slowly but Surely
Stranger in My Arms
You Don't Even Try

ACKNOWLEDGMENTS

FUZZY AND I HAD A lot of help in writing this book. First, we want to thank Norm Hamlet, the band leader for the Strangers for over forty years, for his help. No one knows Merle Haggard's music better than Norm. He was always willing to check facts for us, and he shared some amazing stories that we have placed in the book. Ray McDonald was a close associate of Merle's for many years, and several of his stories are also found in this book. Marty Haggard, Merle's oldest son, shared stories with us that only Merle's family could possibly know. Bob Price has written the definitive book on the Bakersfield Sound, and was a constant source of information for us.

Larry O'Dell with the Oklahoma Historical Society came to Bakersfield and interviewed several Bakersfield Sound musicians and singers who have Oklahoma roots. In many ways, this book grew out of those interviews, which are now in the video archives at the Oklahoma Historical Society in Oklahoma City. Lillian (Haggard) Rea, Merle's sister, was always willing to answer our questions, and she shared with us several stories. Rick Stevens, band-leader for the Bakersfield-based Buck Fever Band, has been a real encourager to get this project done. Rick knows almost every Merle Haggard and Buck Owens song by heart. Pastor Larry Wood of the Valley Baptist Church in Bakersfield assisted in the research for this book. Larry has ministered to numerous people associated with the Bakersfield Sound over the past twenty years. He knows the people and the music of Bakersfield as well as anybody I know. Larry's favorite line from a Merle Haggard song is:

> *I grew up in an oil town*
> *But my gusher never came in!*

I also want to thank Lisa Wysocky, who did our editing and book design, and really made this project come to life. Last, but certainly not least, is my personal assistant, Roseanna Sanders, who typed, and made numerous suggestions for this book.

Thank you all, each and every one.

—Phil Neighbors

I WANT TO THANK MY family, who put up with me as I travelled on the road with Merle for over fifty years. They are:

My wife Phyllis.

My sister-in-law Sherrell Gamboa, her husband Al, and my sister-in-law Ramona Copeland.

My daughter Cindy, and her husband Clint Black-hawk, and my daughter Robin, and her husband Calvin Martens.

My grandchildren, Carly and Casey Ploeger, Cristen and Chad Schaeffer, and John Blackhawk—and my great grandsons Cylus Schaeffer, and Liam and Jude Ploeger

I also want to also thank Merle's family for all their love and support through the years. This includes Merle's wife Teresa, and all of his children.

—Fuzzy Owen

Above: I was just getting started back in Arkansas when this photo was taken.

Below: My cousin Lewis Talley and me in the early days in Bakersfield.

Above: (l-r): Me (fourth from left), Lefty Frizzell, Cliff Crawford, and Ray Price.

Below: Hard to see in this old photo, but it is of a young Merle and his first wife, Leona Hobbs.

A publicity head shot of Bonnie. She was just as beautiful inside as she was outside, and it is easy to see why so many people loved her.

Below: In the studio with Porter Wagoner, Lewis Talley, me, and Merle—with a few others at the board at a recording session in Nashville

Above (standing l-r): Lewis Talley, me, Merle, Bonnie, and Porter Wagoner.

Below: Merle loved to record, and seems happy with what he is hearing!

Above (l-r): Porter Wagoner, Jeannie Seely, Merle, Bonnie, and Ronnie Reno.

Below: Cliff Crawford, me, and Johnny Cash.

Above Tennessee Ernie Ford presents Merle with an ACM award.

Below: Merle, me, and Jack McFadden (Buck Owens manager) at the ACM Awards.

Bonnie at the ACM Awards show.

 MERLE HAGGARD and TUFFY Merle Haggard Enterprises
1950 Collier Avenue
Redding, CA. 96003

I met legendary newswoman Barbara Walters at the Kennedy Center Honors event.

My wife Phyllis and her dear friend Bonnie Owens.

Bonnie and Merle's last photo, taken on the day he sang for her at her memory care center home.

Above: Paul McCartney, Merle, Merle's wife Theresa Haggard, me, and Ben Haggard the night Merle was honored at the Kennedy Center.

Below: Another photo from our big night at the Kennedy Center. L-R: Theresa Haggard, Merle, Paul McCartney, and my wife, Phyllis.

Above: With Paul McCartney at the Kennedy Center Honors.

Below: Me, in front of the restored Haggard box car home at the Kern County Museum in Bakersfield. I think Flossie Haggard would be pleased that her favorite home has been preserved.

Above: I can't tell you how much mail or how many royalty checks I have picked up at PO Box 842 over the decades.

Below: With Merle's son Noel at Merle's celebration of life in Bakersfield.

Above: With Merle's son Ben.

Right: This plaque hangs in the downtown post office in Bakersfield.

THIS BUILDING IS NAMED

IN HONOR OF

MERLE HAGGARD

BY AN ACT OF CONGRESS

PUBLIC LAW

115-140

MARCH 20, 2018

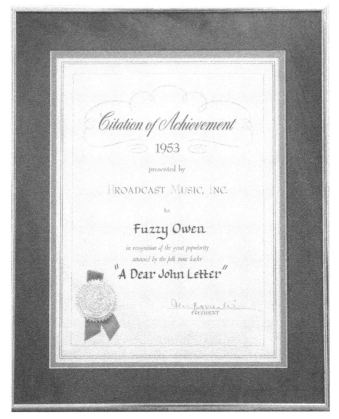

This is the song that started it all. It is amazing to think that without this song, there may never have been a Bakersfield Sound or a legendary songwriter named Merle Haggard.

Some of our many, many gold records.

Above: Just a few of the hundreds of awards the Strangers earned over their long career. Merle deservedly was given hundreds of awards.

Below: Norm Hamlett standing in front of the nine band of the year awards that the Strangers received.

Merle plays his fiddle just like his dad.

CPSIA information can be obtained
at www.ICGtesting.com
Printed in the USA
LVHW091122211219
641329LV00002B/107/P